SWC
MAR 1 2 2002

FIC Hall
Hall, Russ.
Island /

PALM BEACH COUNTY
LIBRARY SYSTEM
3650 SUMMIT BLVD
WEST PALM BEACH, FLORIDA 33406

Also by Russ Hall

World Gone Wrong

The Blue-Eyed Indian

Wildcat Did Growl

ISLAND

by

Russ Hall

Tropical Press
Miami, FL

Copyright © 2001 by Russ Hall

Library of Congress Cataloging-in-Publication Data

Hall, Russ
    Island/ Russ Hall   1st ed

    P.   Cm.
ISBN: 0-9666173-6-3

    1. Hall, Russ
1. Title:

LCCN: 2001087468

All rights reserved, including the rights to reproduce the book, or parts thereof, in any form, except for inclusion of brief quotes in a review. This is a work of fiction, similarities to places and persons alive or deceased is coincidental.

    Cover Design: Dan Frasier
    Cover Photo: Kim Wickwire
    Tuquoise Net (www.turq.com)

Manufactured in the United States of America

TROPICAL PRESS
P.O. Box 161174
Miami, FL 33116-1174
(www.tropicalpress.com)

To become wise, one must wish to have certain experiences and run, as it were, into their gaping jaws. This, of course, is very dangerous; many a wise guy has been swallowed.

-Nietzche

Island

Chapter One

The wind tugged back at my short salt-and-pepper hair. I looked over at the red-and-white striped lighthouse that told us we were nearing Hope Town. Elbow Cay stretched along on the starboard side. It's jagged shoreline took the beating from the white waves at the edge of the blue water as it had for thousands of years. The knife points of hard-as-lava limestone had lost none of their sharp edges. Green began shortly above – sea grape leading up to clusters of swaying coconut palms, occasional stands of Australian and Norfolk pine.

Behind us, a mile across on the other side of the white-capped waves of the sound, a low dark fist of a cumulonimbus cloud hovered with dark gray slanting lines coming down to meet the water. On the horizon a black line of cloud cover was rising. In Hope Town's direction the sky was still clear, but the wind was at our back and rising.

Chancy stood gripping the wheel, staring ahead in relaxed concentration, as focused as some unabashed Ahab close on the trail of his whale. He was tall, and clenched the wheel as if he meant to get someplace. In school he had lettered in football, boxing, and nearly every other sport. I had the one letter in wrestling. I was built closer to the ground.

The white wake spraying out from both sides of our rented 22-foot boat lowered as Chancy backed off on the throttle. He swung the boat around the point and lined up between the red buoy on the right, the green on the left that led up to the yacht harbor – or harbour as they spell it here. The little town of Hope Town lined the left side – the lighthouse, a bait shop, Club Soleil, and a house or two the right. Sailboats, catamarans, and a couple of houseboats bobbed at their moorings across the span of the water that was just as blue as that of the sound we had left. Small flags on their sterns and mast tops rippled in a breeze. Many of them were the blue, yellow, black of the Bahamian flag. Others were from the U.S., Panama, even one from Switzerland.

Chancy slowed the boat and slipped the engine into reverse as we pulled up to the wooden pilings and extended deck of the Harbour's Edge, where I had pushed for us to have lunch. We had been off in the house by ourselves enough that I had a craving to see other people talk, and interact. I had been painting a mental picture of us to Chancy, our being out at one of the picnic tables on the deck doing a bit of people-watching while we had our conch fritters, a couple of cold Becks, and for me a cheeseburger. I knew Chancy would stay with his usual grouper sandwich.

"Yo, throw a stern anchor rope out there, mate!" one of the guys back in the bar yelled at us.

I was turning a couple of half-hitches over one of the posts with the boat's tender. I glanced over their way. It was dark back under the bar, though they could see out across the outside tables and all the way across the harbor.

Chancy didn't say anything. He was just coming around the console and had to turn and go back to throw out the stern anchor. I don't know why he had forgotten this once. We had the drill down pat, had done it dozens of times. It was to keep the back end of parked boats from banging into other boats.

Chancy must have been still looking along the shore again for a taxidermy sign. We had never found one in all the years we had been coming down to the same Hope Town area on Elbow Cay. That had been bothering him. He is the kind of guy who rarely travels anywhere without knowing where a taxidermy shop is located. I always tell him, "If I ever catch anything really huge, throw it back and have me stuffed and mounted on my wall."

He shot past me at a pretty good clip and was already in the darkened back bar area while I was looking around for a place to sit among the Harbour's Edge tourist lunch crowd. All the tables were busy.

I paused to watch a lady who wore a chartreuse and puce Hawaiian shirt throw bits of conch fritter to swirling schools of gray snappers that lived beneath the dock's pilings. The fish were like piranhas, rushing at each scrap, the bigger fish bumping the smaller ones to the side. For the better part of half a plate of fritters torn into bite-size pieces I stood shoulder to shoulder among a press of other tourists and watched the thick-lipped gray fish swirl and thrash. I heard and didn't hear the shouting coming from the darker back section of the restaurant's bar.

When it finally came through to me that something was going on back there, I nudged my way through the others who lined near the edge of the deck. I wove through the tables until I was in the shadows that contrasted with the glaring sun of the umbrella-topped tables on the deck. Back in the dimmer bar portion of the place it took a moment or two for my eyes to adjust. Then I saw Chancy standing very close to a man who stood with his back to the bar. Chancy's hands clutched the man's wrists. Their faces were very close together.

"I know about the bloody back anchor," I heard Chancy saying between clenched teeth. He sometimes affects being British when he is upset. I don't believe that makes him an Anglophile, perhaps just the opposite.

"He was just helpin' out," a fellow said who still sat on his bar stool. He held a long-neck bottle of Beck's in one gnarled fist, and did not look eager to stand up.

"Maybe we didn't need his help."

"There's that," the man at the bar agreed. The one Chancy was gripping said nothing. He was slim, boot-leather tanned and stringy. His eyes were locked with Chancy's – though Chancy, at six-two, had a few inches on the fellow. The man wore a stained white t-shirt, jeans, and oversized black rubber boots that went up to his shins.

I went to the end of the bar where there were two empty stools. In a moment Chancy came over and slid onto the one beside me. I could hear Chancy trying to slow his breathing. The bartender was just sliding the two beers I had ordered in front of me. Chancy reached and took one, tilted it back until it was half gone. As he lowered the bottle back to the bar he said, "Don't know why I was even bothering with him."

A sideways glance caught the two fellows Chancy had been entertaining with their heads close together. Not plotting, I guessed, or hoped, just commiserating.

"Tables are all full," Chancy said, glancing out across the sun-splashed deck where the solitary waitress hurried with a tray toward one of the picnic tables.

"Let's give it a few minutes," I said.

"Can we order here?" Chancy called over to the bartender.

When he had finished pouring a draft beer and mixing some sort of rum punch beverage that involved a chunk of pineapple and a tiny umbrella, he came down to our end of the bar, wiping his hands on a towel. He slid a couple of menus in front of us.

"What's your hurry? Let's wait and eat outside," I said.

"Do I order from you, or do we have to get the waitress back here?" Chancy yelled to the bartender.

I stood up, slipped enough money in Bahamian bills onto the bar for the beer, and went out the back door out onto the sidewalk. I'd gone past only three or four of the houses when Chancy came hurrying up beside me rubbing the back of one hand across his mouth. "You didn't finish your beer. Where're you off to?"

"Have to buy that new gaff. Remember?"

Out on the white sand Tilloo Bank flats Chancy "'Cuda" Phillips had wrestled with a five-foot barracuda for twenty minutes. We had spotted it as a shadow along a submerged dune, and had cast jigs at it until it hit on Chancy's line. He got it to the boat. I gaffed it and held it against the side of the boat while Chancy tried to rescue his jig. We had dozens of jig heads with us. They cost very little, but he was going at it like a surgeon, or dentist, when the 'cuda gave a surge and lunged at my hand that held the gaff. I had dropped it, the line breaking as the fish plopped back into the water. The gaff had fallen and lay four feet down on the white sand. I could see it as clearly as the bright orange starfish beside it. I could also see the 'cuda only ten yards away, still and resting by the closest dune.

"Looks like you'll have to go in after it," Chancy had said, looking down at the gaff.

"I'll spring for a new one," I said. I was watching the 'cuda, who seemed to be watching us. They have a wily intelligence, even though they can be tricked into hitting at a lure like a cat with a piece of yarn. This one looked more rested than I would have liked, and seemed to have copped a bit of an attitude somewhere along the line. "I'll buy a new gaff," I repeated.

Beside us as we walked, thick bursts of bougainvillea

in bright pinks and purples lined the Hope Town wooden fences – the stubby thorns more of a coincidence than any sort of defense system. I turned up a narrow path marked "Lover's Lane." Two young black natives swept at the fallen magnolia leaves in the path ahead of us. One did not stop sweeping, nor did he look up at us. We had to step around him. The other did stop and stepped to the side of the path. He gave us his unblinking and unsmiling stare as we passed.

"There's going to be trouble here some day," Chancy said.

I was looking up at the sky. A black line of solid clouds was lifting above one horizon. The growing patch was darker than an old bruise, more threatening.

We passed Vernon's grocery and bakery. He was also the pastor of the little Methodist church, and had married quite a few couples up in the top of the lighthouse. But he'd seen his share of tourists as well. A sign above the register in his store proclaimed, "Summer people. Some ain't."

"Tell me again," Chancy said, keeping pace with me even though I was walking fast, "how you came to invite someone to go with us."

"It's just for the afternoon."

"A guy you met at the bar?"

"While you were busy entertaining wifey I slipped down to shoot some pool."

"Taking separate vacations. What's that tell you?" he said. His wife was along for the trip, spent her days shopping and laying by the pool with a paperback novel. I figured that was one reason, the main one, that drove him to want to be out on the water prowling all day as if there was a white whale somewhere with his name on it instead of discovering that the island had something of a social life, however primitive in spots. My wife was catching a few shows at Vegas with some of her lady pals, or so she had said.

"I was telling this fellow about the black-tip shark you caught over at Snake Cay," I said. "He says to me, 'I tink I like to catch a shark.' I had to invite him along after that."

"After too many beers, sounds like to me."

When we made it back to the Harbour's Edge there were plenty of picnic tables open. I lay the gaff on the table while the waitress brought us a couple of cold ones. The gaff had a short wooden handle, its razor-tipped chrome hook covered by a protective plastic tube.

"You working a double shift, Monique?" I asked when she put the two bottles on the table. Her full lips lifted in an easy smile. She had butterscotch tanned skin, long blond hair. Her smile had a way of tugging the corner of her lip up, in a way that could have been an Elvis sneer if she had not shown such a benign glow while chewing gum behind it.

"Some have to work," she said. "Wish I could go fishin' with you fellas."

"Surprised he hasn't already asked you," Chancy said. "He asks everyone."

"Sure seems you fellas have the life," she said while scribbling on her pad. "Just fishin' and drinkin'. But I know I only see you on your vacations. Not fair of me to judge."

"That's us," Chancy said. "Tossing back bon bons, living the good life. La dolce vita."

When she headed back to the counter with our food orders he said to me, "On a first name basis with the help, huh."

A woman at the next table was saying loudly to her

female companion, "That house's worth $250,000, book value. How he thinks...."

"What'd the judge say?" her companion asked, all this loud enough for people across the harbor to hear.

"Say? Why, he goes, 'Did you at any time work?' 'Work?' I says, 'I lived with that man eleven years. If that isn't work....'"

"She was working last night," I told Chancy. "I wouldn't read a whole lot into it."

"You ever notice," he asked, "how you've spent the past dozen years being attracted to women who resemble Hanna?"

"Monique doesn't..."

"That hint of recessive chin, the stiff backward thrust of her neck, how slender she is."

"You can't say that Dot fits that pattern," I said. I lifted the bottle clenched in my fist, found it to be empty. I waved the empty bottle at Monique. She held up two fingers back at me, palm outward (which matters in a British-influenced area). I nodded.

Monique looked young, compared to myself and Chancy, that is. She seemed island raised, born here or come early enough to have developed an islander's contempt for we ugly Americans.

Maybe I was reading her wrong. Not that it mattered. What did I care whether she tumbled for a mid-life bit of crust like me. It was just that she was either very aware of her youth or oblivious to it. I had seen the model often enough in the states – that cocksure arrogance of the young. Nurtured and sheltered, they live some rock and roll sense that they will be young forever, that time will never steal the taut lines of their bodies. They look at you with barely suppressed contempt, that idiotic confident sparkle in their eyes, like the way they learned everything was the right way, and your way isn't. When I was as young I had seen the same look often enough (in the mirror) to know it now.

"How are things with you and Dottie?" Chancy asked.

"Fine."

Monique brought the tray of sandwiches with the two beaded bottles of beer. Chancy grabbed at his grouper sandwich and took two rapid bites. After a couple of quick chews and a swallow of beer, he mumbled, "This Rolf, whatever, had better be here before we finish lunch. We can't wait for him."

"Why?" I said.

Chancy kept eating as fast as he could, splashing ketchup on his fries, shoving those in two and three at a time between bites of his sandwich.

"Separate vacations," he said abruptly between bites of his sandwich. He snorted.

I took a bite of my cheeseburger. The bread was very good. The locals make wonderful bread in the Bahamas, a result I think of everything having to be shipped in. They can do something with flour at least. Above us, patches of small black clouds would bunch, then scatter. The black line that had worried me earlier was gone, but the gusting wind had picked up. We sat in the island's lee, but out in the harbor the small flags on the moored yachts stood straight out at right angles, dipping only briefly. I could only imagine what the wind was like out on the ocean side, where we were going.

"Hey, there's Rolf," I said, stood up to wave to him.

He had just come around the building and was rolling across the deck toward us in a walk that was somewhere between John Wayne and Popeye. He had short, blondish gray hair, and was about six-two – the same height as Chancy. But Rolf was all torso, thick upper body on short, slightly bowed sailor's legs. He carried a bit of extra weight too, some in a round paunch, some in his face as well. His rounded reddish cheeks pushed his eyes into narrow twinkling slits. He had a small gray mustache. As a snotty kid I had seen a fellow wearing a shaving brush in his hat who could have been Rolf's twin. I had the kind of ideas then that a mere kid might have that close to the end of World War II. I said some things then that I was much later sorry I had said. The man had not been wearing lederhosen and thick knee socks or anything. I had no way of ever taking those words back.

When I first ran into Rolf at the bar he seemed enough like that man to be his ghost. His eyes, even when sparkling in laughter, held some of that same glimmer of world sadness I remembered all too well.

"By yumping Jack bald-headed Christ," Rolf said as he got to our table, "I'm glad you don't leave without Rolf." He smiled, held out a hand to Chancy. "You're 'Cuda Chancy, I bet."

Chancy took a moment to wipe his hand on a napkin. Then he half stood to shake the extended hand. A reluctant, but genuine smile spread across his face.

Rolf plopped onto the picnic table seat beside me, facing Chancy. He looked at the dozen or so other tourists on the deck around us.

"D'jew eat yet?" Chancy said past a mouthful.

Rolf was glancing away. It sounded like he said. "Yop." His head swung back to Chancy. "Halstead," he said. "It's Rolf Halstead."

"He's a pilot of those boats that pass through the locks of the Panama Canal," I said.

"Is that German?" Chancy asked Rolf.

"He's from Norway," I said, "originally. But he's a U.S. citizen now."

"And can speak for himself," Chancy said. His head swung slowly to me. He turned back to Rolf. "You ever captain any of those really big boats, the tankers, the aircraft carriers?"

"Half to," Rolf said. "Need to be cleared for all classes of vessel. Is why they pay me the big buck." He laughed, to himself.

"A beer, Rolf?" Monique asked. She had appeared beside the table like some rabbit out of a magician's ratty top hat. Rolf nodded.

"You a part of the bachelor's club that hangs out here evenings?" Chancy asked.

There was a silence. I hesitated, but Rolf was watching two young couples get off a boat. They were having an awkward time of it.

"Divorced," I said. "From his third wife. She shot a rifle through the front door, nearly hit two policemen who were beating on the door."

"Cost me half a million," Rolf said, swinging back to Chancy. He said it like it was an amount he might have left in his other pants. But I knew it had changed his retirement plans. It had extended his career by another ten years. "I was her fourth husband. She was a Latin, had hot blood, by tam Christ. She drank. Too much she drank." He leaned closer, lowered his voice, "I tell you. I did one thing wrong, by geez-tam. I should have gone to her, said 'I get you out of this mess.' She think she shoot at me. Drunk, you know. That's all. I should have been on her side then. Maybe I have my half million."

He leaned back and laughed again. "No more women for me. I get a goat next time. You know old story – wear boots to cliff, put back hooves into boots. . . ."

"I had you figured for more of a sheep man," Chancy said.

Monique was in the middle of putting Rolf's beer in front of him, but that didn't phase him. "Nope. A goat for me next time. That's the way to go. What do you tink?" he turned to me.

That getting virgin wool was going to become tough. I said nothing.

"Don't ask him about women, or domestic animals," Chancy cautioned. "A line isn't forming at his door for worldly advice."

I kept my mouth closed by taking a sip of beer.

Rolf nodded to the kids who had come off the boat that sported a red-and-white diving flag." Tourists," he snorted. "Some barracuda sees those flashing diamond earrings on that one and she will be Van Gogh. Right now, you betcha."

"We all have a bit of tourist in us," I said. I was looking at the thick gold Rolex Rolf wore on his wrist. "Even those of us who have been coming down here a couple of times a year."

"You two work for the same place, eh?" Rolf asked.

"Same place, same wonderful boss. V.P. Sid 'the brick' Appleblan," Chancy said.

"Not a nice guy?"

"Don't count on him to suck the poison out if you ever get snake bit." Chancy rubbed his face with a napkin and pushed his empty plate away.

"As assholes go," I said, "he's the total package. He thinks we should be more aggressive," I said, "should compete more against each other. There's one new slot open, and we both have to knock heads for it. The guy who doesn't get it is probably out on his ear." I shrugged. "Just the way it is."

"But you're friends. Why?"

"It's the way things are done back in the city. You

have to know how the system works. That's all," Chancy said. "Now, are we going fishing, or talk all day?"

"You two know what you're doing, don'tcha?"

"We rent from you every year, sometimes twice a year," Chancy said. He was staring at the row of rentals. He pointed to a 22-foot Albury. "They're custom-made by a family over on Man-O-War," he told me.

"I got an 18-foot Whaler. Only a year old if you'd rather."

"We'll take this one," Chancy said.

I watched it bob in the clear water of its dock. I could see a large orange starfish on the bottom below it. The name on the back of the boat was "Pair-O-Dice."

Chapter Two

We swung by the marina bait shop at the mouth of the harbor for more frozen blocks of chum. The gas pump jockey nodded toward our boat. "You going out in that? There's a piece of weather out on that ocean."

"Got to," Chancy said. "Couldn't find any sharks on the sound side."

Rolf and I sat up front as Chancy steered us around the turn past Tilloo Bank that led to Tilloo Cut. The sky was darker out over the ocean. We could see it as a brooding scowl when we looked out through the gap. The waves seemed to be stacking up. I glanced at Rolf's watch. We had an hour or so until high tide. Out on the ocean there looked to be waves from four to six feet, with swells nearly as high farther out. The waves pushing into the narrow cut looked twice as high from here.

"Do you think. . .?" I started to yell back to Chancy.

"You fellows'd better come back here for this," Chancy shouted. The ocean was growling at us like an unfriendly tiger. "You want to put out a line?" he said to me. "See if we get anything on the troll out?"

"Sure," I said. I slid one of my rods out of the holders. I'd rigged it with a trolling jig – round three-quarter ounce red head with eyes, a contrasting chartreuse shrimp tail. I dropped the jig into the water and played out line as we moved into the frothing water toward the narrow neck of the cut. Waves were sure stacking up. When I had enough line out I clicked the reel's free spool closed and held on with one hand. I clasped my free hand around the chrome rail that ran down the side of the center console.

"You want to fish, going true tis?" Rolf said.

There was no time to respond. The boat dipped down into the belly of the first wave and as quickly began to climb up a froth-topped wall of water coming at us.

Chancy stood at the center of the console. He clenched the wheel and the throttle. Rolf gripped the rail on the other side. I looked back, and saw the jig skipping above the crests of waves behind us like a flying fish. I didn't want to think about what we would do if a fish hit the lure. Chancy's face was pinched, his eyes narrowed. The boat got to the top of the wave. We could see the next one building twice as tall.

A sizable slap of saltwater washed over the bow at the very top of the wave, pushing the bow down as we started down into the dip. The coming wave towered over us. A wash of saltwater swept ankle-deep across our feet.

"Hit the bilge pump," Chancy said between his teeth.

I glanced at Rolf. He made no move. I had to let go of the rail and squat down in the bobbing boat to flip the switch that was housed as far back in as I could reach inside the console.

I stood up in a lurch that pitched me toward the gunwale. I grabbed at my rail, barely caught it as the boat slammed into the bottom of the wave's wall. The entire wave slapped down onto us like a giant salty fist.

I could see nothing. My only link with reality was where my hands clenched the rod and rail, and where my spread feet pressed against the deck. Otherwise, it was like being underwater.

We bobbed suddenly out of the water. I blinked the salt out of my eyes as soon as I could, and saw we were already starting up a wave taller than the last. Water poured off every drenched bit of me. Rolf and Chancy were just as soaked. Both stared up at the next wave.

I felt all my weight shift to the hand that gripped the rail. The boat climbed up the wave, tilting, more to the vertical with each foot we rose until we finally were as straight up and down as we could get. The weight of the boat began to make us slip backward down the wave. At that moment I knew we were going to flip over. None of us wore life vests, not that it would have mattered if we did. The boat was going to land on us.

We were straight up and down, the wall of wave stretching out in a blue-green sheen on either side of us, the crest looming and poised to crash down on us as we flipped. I saw Rolf's hand reach over and slip under the hand Chancy held clasped to the throttle. Rolf shoved the hand up and the boat's engine roared with the surge of gas. The bow climbed forward, cut through the top of the wave, and the boat lifted and levelled as we rose and started down the other side.

We rode out the next three smaller waves in the set with Chancy staring ahead, his teeth locked so tight he couldn't speak. He took us out a mile from the shore until we bobbed in swells that ranged from three to five feet. Chancy turned off the ignition key and spun to face Rolf. Before he could speak, Rolf said, "Yumping great Christ on a roller skate. By tam, that was close. Sorry I bump your hand, 'Cuda Chancy. You are sure one cool skipper, I tell you what."

Whatever Chancy was going to say never got said. It seemed very quiet on the boat for a moment. There was the sound the ocean makes as in its regular rising and falling it seems to breathe. Far off there was the "kree, kree" of a gull. I could see the tiny white and blue squares of houses in the green line that was all we could see of the land from here. Chancy turned to me, his face flushed. My heart was pumping a bit too. I realized one hand was a white-knuckle fist around the console rail, the other clenched tight enough to leave indentation marks on the rod handle, I suspected, if I could let go enough to look.

"You ever notice how much the islands out here are like Chia pets – rocks with plant life springing out all green and mysteriously clinging?" I said.

"And just as tacky," Chancy said. "Let's get some lines in the water." To me he added, "You want to take care of getting the chum slick going?"

An abrupt slam jerked my left hand and arm hard enough to nearly yank the rod away if my grip had not bonded the rod to me. I had forgotten the jig dropping through the water behind us.

"Fish on," I yelled.

I managed to wrench my right hand free of the console and turned to start cranking my Penn bait-caster reel. The drag sounded as the fish surged against the tug of the line. I felt the fish's head shake, like a bass – definitely not one of the queen triggerfish we catch so often. The triggerfish have a flat, sideways fighting style.

I cranked away, gaining line until the fish got near enough to see the boat. Then it took off in earnest. I put a thumb down on the level-winding spool to help the drag, adding enough pressure until my thumb felt warm.

The fish stripped out fifty more yards before it turned and I could gain back line. I got it close enough to the boat for us to see the brown and tan mottling of its sides.

"Nassau Grouper," Chancy called out. "Get the gaff." To me he yelled, "Don't play it too long. That's supper. We don't want a shark or 'cuda to get that one."

Rolf stood beside me, the exposed hook of the gaff gleaming in his hand.

The grouper pulled away, but I lifted the rod tip and horsed it back to the boat's side. I swept the rod in a tighter arc while reeling. The big grouper was close to the boat's side. Rolf's left hand dipped, the gold of his Rolex watch glittering in the sun. With a twist of his wrist he sank the gaff under the grouper's chin and lifted. He hoisted the fish onto the deck and let it drop. It lay there, at least twenty pounds, its gills lifting and falling.

Chancy lifted the top of the seat behind the console where we had two large blocks of ice in with the chum and bait. Rolf dropped the grouper in once I got the jig out of its lip.

"A good start," Chancy said. "Good thing we hadn't chummed yet, wasn't it."

I nodded, remembering a queen triggerfish, with skin tougher than a tax collector's heart, that a barracuda had sliced in half as clean as a razor buzz saw. I had been reeling away, had felt the hit, and then felt the fight go out of the triggerfish. I'd let the remaining half drop back down, had gotten another hit, and then I did have a fight on my hands. I got that five-foot 'cuda up to the boat before we cut the line.

"You want to be careful, you clean that one," Rolf said. He nodded to where the grouper was stowed. It was thumping around a bit. "Grouper have a worm, Lernaeenicus sprattae, Hysterothyla-cium aduncum, or Vibriosis – one of those – brown with a silver head. I may not half the name just right, but by tam you find them in the fillets, sure ting."

"You know," Chancy said, as he lifted one of the blocks of chum out of the well and slipped it into a nylon net bag, "your Latin is better than your English. I thought your area of expertise was goats." He lowered the chum bag into the water and tied off the line on one of the cleats.

Rolf didn't respond. He took the rod I handed him, and reached for a chunk of the ballyhoo I was cutting.

"Soon as that chum begins to thaw and break up, we should see some 'cuda action," Chancy said, "maybe a shark or two. The yellowtails'll probably be the first to school around us."

I switched to one of the weighted bait rigs with its steel leader and larger capacity level-wind reel. I had put three hundred yards of new line on the spool. I let out eighty-five feet before I hit bottom. I cranked up a couple of turns on the reel. The rod tip jerked down. I snapped the rod up and set the hook. I got a little fight, but nothing like the grouper. I reeled up a strawberry hind. Rolf was using the pliers to get a five-pound queen triggerfish off his line. Chancy brought a mutton snapper flopping onto the deck. "We keep the snappers," he said. "Throw everything else back, or cut it up and put it in the chum bag, especially any grunts."

I had eaten grunts myself, and found them good. But in Florida once, Chancy had heard someone call the grunt Haitian hamburger. He wouldn't keep them after that.

I didn't have to tell Rolf which was which. He knew all the Caribbean fish as well or better than us. He avoided the sharp edges of the yellowtail's gill covers on the next fish he caught. He slipped it into the well. But he threw back the big-eyed reddish squirrel fish he caught a few minutes later.

I watched for any sign of shark, or barracuda. The oily sheen of the chum slick was beginning to be an obvious line stretching off downwind of the boat.

We drifted in a parallel course and were only slightly nearer the shoreline. In addition to the white and blue squares of the houses, I could make out a dark cluster of buildings. That would be the Abaco Inn. The boat lifted and dropped with the swells. The bobbing did not seem to bother an old seadog like Rolf. But I watched the shoreline more and caught myself swallowing. I fancied I could smell gas fumes from the engine, though it had been turned off a while.

"Holy tam frying pan," Rolf said. He lifted half of a hind into the boat. Something had bitten off the back half.

"Put it back in," Chancy shouted. "Whatever hit it will come back."

Rolf lowered the half-eaten fish back down. Nothing took off with it. He waited a few minutes, then reeled up and rebaited.

Rolf not getting a shark on seemed to put Chancy in good spirits. He said, "What kind of bird is that over there, Nature man?"

"Frigate," Rolf said.

"To hell with you too." Chancy was laughing, and Rolf with him, first in chuckles that were hard to stop, easing into that hysterical laugh that starts after there has been some tension.

I was watching the bird with its long wings soaring off higher, riding some ocean thermal. I knew that to tell hawks from vultures you look at the slant of the birds' wings. A bird of prey's wings form a straight line across, a vulture's wings form a slight V. This bird had red at its throat, as if slashed there. The wings were thin bent blades. It had a long forked tail. If it was a sign of something, I didn't know what. I don't know how Rolf knew this bird from the albatross Coleridge's "Ancient Mariner" had worn around his neck.

"Hey, goat man," Chancy said, "you said you'd never caught a shark. You ever catch a barracuda, a really big one?"

"Yust small ones. Ones you can eat." He turned to me. "Once 'cuda get big they get ciguatoxic, make you sick, you eat them. Comes from eating fish that eat poison coral."

"We know about the ciguatera," Chancy said.

Rolf didn't respond.

I was looking at the green line of the shoreline. The wind that was bobbing us and that kept the ocean in white caps was making the taller palm trees sway.

"Still think it looks a helluva lot like a Chia pet," I said.

Rolf gave a silent chuckle.

Chancy looked over toward Elbow Cay. "You know, there's something about a place that survives by tourism that's a lot like the spreading of thighs. What do you think?" He was looking at Rolf.

"I think we had this conversation already," I said, "back in Hope Town. We're tourists too, remember."

"Don't you have any theories on that, goat man?" Chancy wouldn't leave it alone.

Rolf jigged his bait up and down off the bottom, gave it his full attention.

Chancy started to say something but stopped when his rod snapped into an arc. I heard his drag sound as the fish took line.

"Queen?" I asked.

He shook his head. "Fights like a grouper, a big one."

He wrestled with it a good five minutes before he got it close enough to the boat for us to see it before it surged in another run.

"Grouper," I agreed. "A big one."

"Could go thirty pounds," Chancy said.

"It would be a record," Rolf said. "Nassaus only get twenty pounds or so. Record is twenty-seven pounds."

"Listen. . ." Chancy said. He leaned back with his rod, the tip bent quite a ways as he reeled in the stubborn line. He didn't get a chance to finish. His rod snapped suddenly forward. Line began to scream from his reel. He had to lean forward, rod tip down toward the water as the line ripped out.

"Shark?" Rolf asked.

"Or something big," I said.

"Fire the engine," Chancy yelled. "We may have to chase it if its a shark."

Rolf was reaching for the ignition key when we saw the long silver side of a fish swirl deep under us.

"'Cuda," I yelled. "Never mind the engine."

"We may need it," Chancy puffed as he reeled. "It's a big one, could go eight feet."

"Never heard of one over six," Rolf said.

"We'll see, goat man. You may see one soon."

Several times Chancy got the big 'cuda near enough to see the boat, and for us to see it before it spun in a silver flashing bar to strip out line again. I had never heard of a barracuda over six foot either. But this one seemed to be. It was a huge fish, bigger than any I'd ever seen. It had to be to go after a grouper as large as that like it was a bait fish. A couple of times I had to squeeze a cloth of saltwater over Chancy's reel to cool it. Beads of sweat stood out on his forehead. The way he stood told me his back was beginning to ache.

"None over six feet, eh," he grunted. The barracuda was near enough for us to get a good look at it. It could be eight feet, hard to tell. It was the biggest I had ever seen.

We bobbed in the swells while the land eased by us in our slow drift. I looked at my watch early in Chancy's wrestle with the fish. It was thirty-two minutes later when the barracuda seemed spent enough to be drawn to the side of the boat.

"Get the gaff," Chancy called out. "I want a picture."

I went forward to get the camera out of my gear bag.

I pulled myself along the swaying starboard gunwale toward the stern. Rolf had the gaff in hand and was pulling on the steel leader. The head and open jaws of the 'cuda lifted out of the water. Each tooth looked half an inch across at its base.

"Lay his gill against the side," Chancy suggested. "Should cut his breathing."

"I wasn't aware fish could breathe out of water," I said.

"You ready to take the picture?" He was cranking in the last of the line, lifting on the bent rod to help Rolf lift the 'cuda. It was a good eighty to a hundred pounds. I sure was not going to weigh it. Its head and huge eyes lay pressed to the side of the boat, its outside gill lifting and falling in tired gasps. It was one enormous slab of silver muscle and bony head.

Rolf had to use both arms to lift it. When he had it bent over the gunwale, he stepped aside, holding the gaff with his left hand. Chancy stepped closer for the photo. I got up and stood on the seat behind the console. Through the viewfinder the fish looked smaller. So did Rolf and Chancy. There was nothing small about Chancy's grin. I squeezed the shutter button, heard a splash above the sound of the camera.

The camera dropped and hung by its cord around my neck. I stared at the 'cuda. The splash had been its tail slapping the water as it lunged. Its massive head was a blur heading for Rolf's arm, his shining gold Rolex, or the silver shaft of the gaff. I don't know which. The gaff fell to the deck, made a clatter. The barracuda banged once against the side of the boat and dropped back into the water with a churning splash. Chancy and I were staring at Rolf. Blood began to ooze from the side of his hand. He looked down, saw what we saw. The three end fingers and half his palm were gone.

I was frozen for a second. Some roar of silence filled my ears. As it slowly cleared I heard Chancy say, "That must hurt like dammit."

Blood began to pour out of the hand. I hopped down from the seat and ran to Rolf. Without knowing I was doing it, I tore my shirt up the front and had a strip ready as I got to him. I grabbed his wrist and began to bind the cloth around his arm as a tourniquet. I used the pliers to twist the cloth down until it tightened and stopped the bleeding. I held it in place and stretched to my bag, yanked out my tiny first aid kit from the side pocket. I had half a dozen SteriStrips. I used them all to pull the wound closed. Then I used up the butterfly suture bandaids to finish the rest. I tore another strip from my shirt and wrapped it around before I loosened the tourniquet. It seeped red at once. I tore apart the rest of my shirt and bound the rest of the strips around Rolf's hand. I used up the small roll of tape to hold the whole mess in place.

"Tam, oh tam, oh tam," he said. His pink face was washed pale. He stared down in shock at the mitten I was making around his hand.

"Tam," Rolf said. "Oh, tam."

"You just go on your damned vacation!"
"Why don't you come, Dot?"
"And sit while you and that Chancy chase sharks or any other damned thing with teeth? Don't the two of you get enough of that at the office."
"We could. . . ."
"Go to Treasure Cay shopping? Snorkel over the reefs? Swim with the dolphins? You promised all that last time. You want to go off with that Chancy, you go. Just go."

Chapter Three

Chancy stood, mouth part open, taking deep breaths. He watched for a bare moment, then spun and rushed to the console, fired up the motor.

Rolf and I bounced on the deck as the boat cut through the waves heading back toward the cut. I finished wrapping the hand, using up what was left of my shirt. I was sorry not to have anything left I needed to do. Rolf's breathing had settled a bit. He stared down at the thick wad of cloth around his hand, at the smears of blood on the deck and up his forearm.

I stood and held the rail, moved to the front where I could get my spare t-shirt out of my bag. The smell of the salt air, a fishy edge to it now, filled me. I stood, looked to the approaching black jagged gates of rock on either side of the cut, the white plumes of sea spray shooting up thirty feet into the air as the waves pressed and crashed into the cut. The tide would be rising still, coming in through the cut. Going back through, though, would be nothing like going out.

Land was close enough I could make out the windows of the houses, their slanted wooden shutters tilted out from the tops, propped with sticks to let the breeze in and cool them against the sun that was beginning to bear down on us. I had not noticed the cloud cover breaking up, but it was gone. I looked out across the sea, saw no ships or boats in any direction.

"Hang in there, Rolf," Chancy said. "We'll get you there."

It was quiet from where Rolf still sat on the deck. He had not risen to sit on the cushioned front seat. I realized

I had been finding reasons to look around, anywhere but at him.

"Why no 'goat man' now?" Rolf said.

"What?" Chancy was staring ahead as we entered the cut. The first wave lifted us fifteen feet. We rode its crest, Chancy gunned the throttle and backed off to keep us on the tops of the waves.

"Why don't you call me goat man no more? Now it's Rolf. 'We get you in, Rolf.' Where did 'goat man' go?"

Rolf's face was flushed. He held himself up with his good hand, his other swathed one laying across his lap like a small child. He was getting louder, seemed to be working himself into a lather.

"Why don't you stay close to Rolf there," Chancy said to me. "See if he needs anything."

"I need my hand back," Rolf shouted. He started to struggle to his feet, panting. "Call me 'goat man' now," he yelled.

"Calm down," Chancy said. The next wave was higher than the first. We lifted up, teetered at the top and shot down the other side, our bow heading toward a dip into the water. Chancy goosed the throttle and the boat levelled out and we started to lift.

"Goat man. Goat man," Rolf screamed. He was on his feet now, not tottering nearly as much as I would have been doing without holding onto anything. I saw he held the gaff in his right hand. He stared at Chancy.

"Now, don't do. . . ." Chancy didn't get to finish. Rolf charged.

The boat bucked as Chancy let go of the wheel. He ran around the console on the starboard side, Rolf coming around at him from the port side waving the gleaming hook. The boat rocked as it turned to its side in the wave. We swayed and I grabbed the console rail, pulled myself around to the wheel. Rolf and Chancy went past me.

The wheel was turning free, spinning, stopping with the way the roll of the waves pitched us. When I grabbed it, the force of its movement slammed me to my left. I wrenched at it, struggling for control, while levering up with my legs for torque. Our boat tilted sideways, the crest of a wave breaking over our side and pouring into the boat. Salt water ran across my ankles. We were parallel to the waves, should have been cutting into them. I yanked the wheel and shoved the throttle up to force our turn. Chancy went by again in a lap around the deck. I caught only a glitter of the hook from the corner of my eye as Rolf followed.

The black wet rocks reared suddenly in front of us as we lifted in the water. The current had taken us to the far right side of the cut, far too close to the jagged edges. I pushed the throttle all the way, and gave the engine all the gas I could. The surge lifted us in a jerking turn to port, away from the rocks, but out of timing with the waves. Another huge slap of saltwater hit us, knocked me to the side, and swept across the deck. I clenched the wheel and throttle, righted myself and blinked away the salt. Chancy slipped, fell to the deck. The steel hook swept toward him in an arc, bounced off the deck as Chancy slithered on the sloshing deck past Rolf's feet. Chancy scrambled to his knees, then feet, took off in the other direction. I had us back in rhythm with the waves just in time for the boat to lift high on the lip of the largest wave yet. That was when Chancy crashed into me, knocking me away from the wheel. The gaff's needle point slashed the air missing us both. My feet slid on the tilting wet deck, and I tumbled toward the transom. Either I slammed into it, or it into me. I went black, hearing shouts, feeling the saltwater slosh around my shoulders on the deck, then nothing.

* * *

My eyes snapped open, fluttered for a moment in the blast of yellow sunlight, stayed open as the sky eased to blue with flecks of cloud or reflecting white caps speckled in random sweeps. A small wave of water swept against my cheek. I tasted salt, a copper metallic flavor with it that came with the throbs inside my skull. I wanted to rise, but lay listening to the rustling and clattering on the boat above the sound of the ocean and wind. Water sloshed against me while the sky swung back and forth.

A shudder rippled through me. Then I decided I would rise. I pushed myself up from the deck with the flat of my hands, sat for a moment until my head floated back like an uncertain balloon. The rustling came from Rolf going through the packs. I looked around the boat, found Chancy sprawled chest down on the deck, his head turned to one side – and what a head it was. His head was as big as a basketball, one open eye bulging from its socket, like some bloodshot ping pong ball.

"Is he. . .?"

"Dead " Rolf said. "No. You hit your head when you fell. Him, I hit with the handle of the gaff."

I ran a hand over my face. It came away sticky. I looked at it for blood.

"Sun block," Rolf said.

"You put any on him?"

"He has bigger problems besides the sun."

I could see that Chancy was breathing now that I looked. Water was two inches deep in the boat. It made small waves against him as the boat rocked.

"No radio. No flare gun. No three-mile whistle." Rolf was still poking through our bags. "How did tis boat get cleared for rental?"

I pulled myself to my wobbly feet. We were quite a ways from the land. Elbow Cay was a thin black line.

"Bilge pump?" I asked.

"Dead. Dead as the engine."

"We're taking on water."

"We are, yah. Hit the rocks back tere when no one was at the helm. I tink we sink soon."

"This boat won't sink. It can't – has floatation material all through the body. It may fill with water, but it won't sink."

"Then we wish we sink." He nodded to the water off the starboard bow. A fin lifted, and beneath it a long black silhouette that seemed as long as the boat. It rose near our boat's side, let us see its long hammer of a head. Farther away the fins of two blacktips showed. "We get your sharks now. Too tam bad 'Cuda Chancy don't catch one."

I grabbed the fillet knife I had been using to cut bait. It was under water by the transom. I slashed at the cord that held the chum bag to the boat. The bag began to settle to the bottom. The fins went beneath the surface.

"Let's get what gear we can save above the water," I said.

Rolf had lifted the bags onto the seats. But they too would soon be covered by water. I went through my bag first. There was not much there that would be bothered by the water, the camera maybe, but I was thinking of survival gear. From that perspective, there was very little in my tackle bag that was worth much of a damn. I reached for Chancy's bag.

"Same ting," Rolf said.

"Guess we didn't count on being adrift at sea," I said. Water was lapping higher on Chancy. "We'd better get him above the water line." I got my arms under Chancy's shoulders and started to lift. He was sure a big sack of flour. I looked up. Rolf was hesitating.

"Tis job you two must compete for. . . ?" he said. "You want tis job?"

"Don't."

"You must be aggressive, your boss says, compete."

"Not like that. Give me a hand with him."

Rolf shrugged. He came over and helped me hoist Chancy up onto the front seat. We took the straps off the tackle bags, used them to strap Chancy upright against the front of the console. His head lolled back and forth with the tossing of the boat. But it would at least be above the water now, no matter how deep the boat filled. I did not like the way the lashings made his arms stick out to the sides – made him look like a crucifix. I went to the back of the boat where I wouldn't have to look at him like that.

Rolf was moving around more than I would have in his place, hurt that bad – hardy sailor stock, no doubt. He set aside spare hooks, some bait, put them on the top of the console. "We may need to fish for food," he said, "later."

I was not hungry.

"You want to eat some grouper?" he asked.

"No."

"Like sushi, " he said. "If you knew sushi, like I knew sushi. . . ." He trailed off into a hum.

I suddenly found his accent as well as his moving around so brisk and cheerful irritating. For a moment I wrestled with that, settled on the idea that it was no different than the smell of the engine bugging me earlier.

"Tell me about tis job," Rolf said. "One you two must compete for."

"Why?"

"Tis competing for a job, it interests me." The blue slits of his eyes glittered at me. He pulled the grouper from the bait well, began to fillet it, holding the fish to the table with the elbow of his hurt hand, running the knife down along the fish's rib cage in a practiced way. Laying the blade between the skin and fillet, pulling until he had a clean chunk of white meat. I doubt if I could have done as efficient a job with both good hands. He cut the thick sides into strips, lay them across the top rail of the console to dry in the sun. He spotted one of the parasites he had mentioned earlier. It was a brown and green string with a silver bullet of a head. He cut it out the way you would the eye from a potato. He flicked it over the side with the tip of the knife. Then he sprinkled saltwater over the drying strips of fish meat to cure them a bit.

"It's a management slot," I said, "overseeing others who do what we do now."

"And you want tis job? Really want to manage people?"

"Well. . .Not really." I had not spent a lot of deep thought on it. It was a step you made or didn't make if you were to stay in the business.

In the far distance I could make out a ship, a huge oil tanker it looked like from here, far enough away to seem tiny. It was in a sea lane – too far to spot or help us.

"You don't strike me. . . ." he said.

"No," I interrupted. "But that's the job. I don't want to manage anyone, or be managed. It's just that I've put in my years for this so far, as Chancy has."

A groan came from the front of the boat. I went up for a look. Being strapped upright seemed to agree with Chancy. The swelling had gone down quite a bit. His head wasn't normal yet, but it was improved, very improved. The swelling in the eye had reduced enough that they were both closed. His breathing was regular. But he was still as out of it as the last heavyweight challenger.

"What are you trying to say?" I pressed, "That I ought to heave him over the side?"

"I didn't say to heave."

He had damn well hinted, I thought. But there was no good to come of pressing it. I went through the supplies we had, concentrated on the water supply. We had a gallon and a half in various places. All of it was filtered water. I tied it all to the top of the console. The sun may hit it, but the saltwater couldn't corrupt it.

We sat in the boat, the water rising slowly around us. I found an empty gallon water jug in the front hatch I could cut into a scoop. I began to bail with it. Rolf used the bottom half of a plastic box that had held cigars in Chancy's bag. He bailed with that. Trying to bail by hand made little sense. But it was something to do. We could only hope for a boat. We stared off at the ocean all around us, bobbing as the day turned from blue to gray. As it got darker, the only sounds above that of the waves and an occasional bird was the splashing of our steady bailing.

The water woke me, and I realized it was dark. Water was up to my chest where I sat. My regular shivering, like a cat purring, was what woke me. The sky was black except for the sprays of stars and the sliver of a moon. I looked for Orion's belt. Rolf was awake at the other end of the boat. There was no sound of bailing. He held his wrapped hand out of the water with his other arm. But I could see the wrapping stained darker even in the dim starlight. The water inside the boat was within a foot of the gunwales. Taller waves shipped water inside as each one slapped against us. Around us I saw the fins, twenty to thirty of them now, circling and circling.

"Chancy, why don't we fly over to Nassau, visit the casinos. It says here. . ."

"You know tomorrow's shark day, Myrna honey. We agreed. You said. . ."

"Any of the guys know you talk like that to me?"

"Look on the other side of that page, Myrna. Article there says the incidents of criminal activity in Nassau have risen significantly over the past few years. Flow of weapons is up, and the Royal Bahamas Police force has been over-matched."

"Why did you buy a paper that's a week-and-a-half old?"

"It's all there was at Vernon's. We're supposed to be cut off from television, radio, the news here."

"We're cut off all right. Says here that in Thailand police estimate that more than a hundred men have been seriously mutilated sexually since 1993 when Loretta Bobbitt started a trend."

"Should I sleep out on the hammock?"

Chapter Four

"Rolf," I said. "You're awake?"

"Yop."

"Not bailing?"

"No. Not bailing."

I ached, could feel every bone in me rattling gently – they were as cold as icy knives. My lips felt stiff and wrinkled when I licked them. I tasted salt and something else I didn't want to name.

"The boat's half full," I said.

"Half full, half empty. Depends on your point of view."

"Don't joke, Rolf. Now's not the time."

"Now is perfect time." I could barely make out his face from across the boat, but he seemed to smile. "Now is best time I can ever tink of."

I heard a groan. Cold as I was, another chill rippled up my spine. I sloshed forward. In what light I could get from the slender moon and stars I saw that Chancy's eyes were open.

"Can you drink some water?" I said.

"Yeah." It was somewhere between a gasp and a croak. As the sun was going down earlier I had noted how red his face had gotten.

I untied one of the smaller water bottles and lifted it to his mouth. "Not too much."

"More," he said. I gave him some more. I was pleased to see that all the swelling had gone. Perhaps the chill air and water had done him some good.

"My arms. What's. . . ?"

"We tied you up earlier."

"Tied me?"

"To keep you from drowning," Rolf said.

"Well, untie me."

I had gotten one of the lashings undone as he said it. He slipped his own arm out of the other side while I was still loosening the strap. He lowered his arms, raised them again, went up and down with them like a wounded bird checking out its systems.

"Be calm," I said.

"What are you talking about?"

I realized I was taking short breaths. Rolf stayed where he was, did not seem to share my caution.

"That's all over," Chancy said. To Rolf he said, "How bad is it?"

"Not good."

"I know the situation stinks. I mean your hand."

"Been better."

"The water's on top of the console," I said. "Some dried grouper fillets too."

He turned to me. In the hazy light his face looked dark and warped, a bit like a reflection is some funhouse mirror. He reached past me for one of the chunks of meat. He took a bite and chewed slowly. "Needs something," he said. "Cocktail sauce, maybe."

Rolf laughed, a painful sounding chuckle.

"Bet Myrna's wondering what the hell," Chancy said. "You're lucky you didn't bring Dot along after all."

"And I'm the lucky divorced one," Rolf said, "the goat man."

"Yeah, the goat man." There was nothing bitter in the way Chancy said it.

"It probably doesn't make a hell of a lot of difference," I said, "but the reason Dot went to Vegas was to get a divorce, I think. I'm pretty sure."

"She was always a good housekeeper," Chancy said. "I suppose she'll keep the house." I could hear him chewing the toughened grouper meat.

Rolf laughed out loud, a hearty roar this time.

Chancy rubbed his hands together for warmth, and began to slosh around until he found one of the small flashlights I had put with what needed saving. He flicked the light around the boat taking his own inventory. "You know, for a seaman, Rolf," he said, "you keep a pretty damp boat."

"Is yust a heavy dew," Rolf said, seemed to find that very funny.

I looked in every direction into the dark around us, but saw no lights from any ships. The light from Chancy's flash flickered behind me.

"I sure never thought. . ." I said. "Oh, hell. I don't even know what matters. Everything I ever cared about's changed anyway. Towns I lived in got crowded. Whole woods I walked in got mowed down or lost their charm. Women got bitter. Roads I used to drive down for fun are seven lanes wide now with bumper-to-bumper traffic." I was shaking pretty hard. Maybe I thought flapping my mouth would help.

"Tings change, kid," Rolf said.

"My father was killed while he was in the military. I was only seven." I couldn't seem to stop. "I remember lots of things, but not what he looked like. The little Ohio town I grew up in doesn't even resemble itself anymore. I've just been going day to day, wondering what the hell is going on. Just what the hell is going on, anyway?"

Chancy found my bailing scoop and the box bottom Rolf had been using to bail. "My cigars?" he said.

"Top of the console," I said.

"Shouldn't be dried out," he said. He found them. I

heard him bite the end off one, spit the end over the side. There was a flicker of light. He puffed at it until he had it going. "Lighter works," he said. "Something to be said for that. Either of you want a smoke."

"You bet," Rolf said.

"Okay," I said. "Sure. It's a lousy time to worry about dying from cancer."

Chancy gave me a hard wet slap on the back. He and Rolf laughed.

While he helped Rolf and I get our cigars going, I noticed that Rolf's wrapped hand dripped a pink drop into the boat.

"Think we should try to wrap that again?" I asked.

"With what? Your wet shirt?" Chancy said.

"Keeps the sharkies happy," Rolf said.

Chancy looked around us. There were only two or three fins moving. We still had company.

"You going to catch a shark now, 'Cuda Chancy?" Rolf said. The glow at the end of his cigar lit his face enough for me to see the grin.

"Why not?" Chancy said. "Why the hell not?"

"I tink he catch one, by geez-tam rocking chair," Rolf said.

"Are you. . .?" But Chancy had grabbed his thickest rod from the holder and had hoisted it dripping and slipped it into one of the rod-holding tubes on the gunwale. He dug among the tackle Rolf had placed on the console, found one of the shark hooks. He began tying it to his steel leader, the cigar sticking up from the corner of his mouth in a jaunty angle.

He grabbed one of the pieces of grouper and slipped it onto the hook. I had watched him hand-sharpen each of the shark hooks into needle points back at the house we had rented and shared for the week. He lifted the rod from its holder and flicked the free spool switch to let out line. "Come on one of you leathery bastards," he said, puffing hard at his cigar. The glow lengthened, lit up his face, and gave him a demonic sharky grin. He clicked the switch, stopping the bait's descent. He began to jig the bait up and down. I saw one of the fins slip below the surface, then another.

All around us the sea was dark. There was not even the glow in the sky of any distant civilization. The stars seemed bright and close enough to reach up and pick. The breeze that swept across us was steady, but not as harsh as before. The cigar tasted very good, almost sweet with each puff. I looked over at Rolf. He held the console rail with his good hand and leaned forward to give Chancy his full attention.

Chancy's shoulders jerked forward and the rod snapped into an arc. Line screeched out against the drag.

"By tam jingo bald-headed Christ, he hook one tam big shark."

I nodded, grinning. Chancy arched his back. Line burned out from his reel. The line cut through the water away from us. "Isn't anyone going to start the engine?" he puffed.

Rolf laughed. I felt the boat moving beneath us. The boat tipped in the direction the shark was taking us. Water shipped in over the transom. "Might not be a bad idea to bail a bit, though," Chancy said. He leaned back against the rod. Line still went out. It was too soon in the run to gain any line back. Chancy let the shark have its run, but made it pay for what line it stripped. The drag got louder as he tightened it.

Rolf and I found our bailing tools and got busy. We moved across the rolling surface of water. The wind that pushed against our faces now came from moving into it.

"You keep up this pace," Rolf said, "I tink I like to water ski." He chuckled while he bailed. He held his wrapped hand above the water. The saltwater must have stung like hell, but it did not keep him from laughing. I found myself grinning too. I chewed on the cigar, puffed, and bailed like a madman.

The boat moved along for a few hundred yards then jerked to a stop. The shark sounded. Line Chancy had fought for ripped back out. The tug of the line was straight down below us. I could see the tip of Chancy's rod jerking back and forth as the shark shook its head. The line lifted, and straightened out. The boat swung and started off in a different direction.

I had no idea which direction we had been going on the first run, and had about as good an idea now.

"West," Rolf said when he saw me looking around. He was looking up at the stars without stopping his bailing.

"That good?" I asked.

"Very."

"Any idea where we are?"

"Atlantic Ocean," he said, and indulged himself with one of his chuckles.

There was an enormous splash a hundred yards from the boat. The shark had breached, like a whale.

I looked that way, but it was over. "You see it?" I yelled at Chancy.

"Of course. Couldn't tell what kind it was, though."

"Keith, the bartender at Rudy's, told me about a bull shark that rammed a fishing boat this size. Cracked it right in half," I said.

"I was there when he told you," Chancy grunted.

The boat was moving along at shark speed again. The fish gave a lunge now and then that stripped out more line.

"Getting it to come toward us," Chancy panted, "isn't

the problem at the moment."

He turned to me. His squinting eyes in his tanned face in the dark were like two burned holes in a weathered ship's sail.

Rolf and I kept bailing. We made a gain on the water coming in through the cracked hull. We each had to wait until the boat tilted to one side or the other in order to get a really good scoop.

My back ached. Rolf grinned and watched Chancy lift his rod and crank his reel.

It was getting lighter. The sky grew gray behind us. I had not checked my watch when Chancy had hooked the shark. But it felt like it had been over an hour. As the light hit him, I could see sweat down the middle of Chancy's back, under his arms. He did not ask for help, and we did not volunteer it.

I had not been keeping track of the line going in, then back out again. When I did get a glance at the reel, I saw that Chancy had gained back most of the line. He was reeling faster. The shark was coming toward us. I dropped my scoop and moved up beside Chancy.

A fin came up out of the water ten feet from the boat. It was the big dorsal fin. Behind it – a lot farther behind it than I would have liked – the caudal fin broke the surface of waves when it swished. I felt, rather than saw, Rolf come up to stand beside us.

"Hammerhead," Rolf said.

The bulky black shadow of the shark's head lifted to the surface. The wide hostile eyes on the outside ends of the hammer of its head swept the boat as if taking its measure. The shark gave a twist and headed down, line screaming from the reel again.

"I think it was Rolf that scared it," I said.

"Probably," Chancy agreed.

"Tat tam fish not scared," Rolf said.

The boat was filling with water faster now in spite of all the bailing Rolf and I had done. To hell with it. We stood and watched Chancy reel in line painfully and lose it again in long bursts. The noise the reel made was harsher. The fish had taken its toll on the working parts. It had taken a toll on Chancy too.

Another twenty minutes went by before the shark was near the boat. The sun had popped up above the horizon looking as large as a world on fire. It settled down to searing us where we stood. Rolf and I rubbed sun block on – me wondering all the while whether it was worth doing. I went to rub some on Chancy's reddening neck, but he shrugged it off.

His rod was bowed, line burrowing in across guides that might be getting grooves from the line going in and out. We had drifted all the while, lost our earlier clutch of sharks, but had found a new batch. I looked at the wrapping on Rolf's hand. It had dried into a caked mess. His wrist was swollen, and I did not want to be the one to open the wrappings if it came to that. So it was not his hand that brought the new sharks, or the chum bag I had cut away.

The white underside of the shark's head lifted abruptly five feet from the boat as it lifted out of the water. Its mouth was open, like a razor-edged frown. The eyes on the ends of the hammer cast around in the shark's leap. Blood ran down from the steel leader at its mouth. That had to be it – what was drawing the other sharks. The shark landed with a whump that threw saltwater across all three of us. The rod jerked forward and Chancy with it. Rolf and I both grabbed at him to hold him on board. He waved us off, kept his feet and stared down to the line zipping into the water while the reel protested.

He had been calm all the way through the fight. Now he got mad, lifted up on the rod and began to reel, fighting the fish with everything he had in him. He gained line back too. The shark was tired – hard to tell how spent with one that large. But the line filled back in on the reel and soon the black body of the hammerhead lifted to the surface, snapping left and right as it tossed his head against the line. It lifted and wagged its head at us.

I looked at the shark's bloodshot eyes. It seemed to see us, take us all in. I saw the Vs in the water as the other sharks came for it, watched the fins lower, saw the jar in Chancy's shoulders as the shark got hit. Each shark flew in, grabbed, twisted it head, and tore at the hammerhead.

At first the line shot out and Chancy put his thumb on the spool until the line was pink going out. When the line slowed, began to drop as the sharks hit again and again, Chancy lifted his right hand. He looked at his bloody thumb and seemed surprised.

The rod continued to bend, from the falling body of what was left of the hammerhead or what I could not see. Rolf picked up the fillet knife. He reached out with his good hand and sliced the line.

Chancy rocked back and settled into place – not mad, not anything. He stared out across the water. I looked where he was looking. A boat was coming our way. It was headed right at us.

The sea around us rose in steeper swells, the glass of the surface broken here and there by a bit of yellow-brown seaweed. Green-blue mounds of water stacked in all directions, nearly cresting at the horizons.

A school of a dozen flying fish rose in sudden and energetic arc, lifting from one steely mound of water to plunge into the next. Their silver sides glittered and the image of their arch lingered in the air in drops of water like the strings of a harp.

Pretty in itself, but then there was knowing that beneath the waves something bigger swam that had inspired the flight, something that wanted to eat them.

Chapter Five

The boat got nearer. "What kind of ship is that?" Chancy asked.

Rolf said, "Frigate."

"No it's not. It's a cutter."

Rolf shrugged, his smile tired and forced.

The tall steel side of the cutter pulled up within fifty yards of us. It looked very gray and business-like in the bright sun that beat down on us. So did the four men who came across to us once they had lowered a smaller boat, a military scarab, or RIB – rigid inflatable boat, as they call them.

Rolf stumbled as he was being helped into the boat first. He looked pale. I sat down in the boat beside him. Rolf's sea legs were too good for him to sway. But he seemed to let go a bit inside now that help was here. He must have lost a quite a bit of blood. It was hard to tell how he was rolling with the shock of his injury. He had been keeping a lot back.

One of the sailors was rigging something to our boat. He hit a switch and a balloon filled and rose, a line from it tied to our boat. "Leave the gear," he told Chancy.

Chancy's mouth opened, closed.

"No room for it. The boat can be salvaged later."

"Maybe," Chancy said.

"Maybe," the sailor agreed.

Chancy quickly pulled the reels from a couple of his rods, and carried these and a handful of his cigars with him as he joined us. The sailor stared at him, impatient and stern. But he said nothing.

"Having never been rescued at sea before," Chancy, "I find your attitude a bit cavalier to my taste." All this in that mock British tone his voice sometimes acquires. "We're U.S. citizens, you know."

"And we are a U.S. Coast Guard vessel, sir," the sailor nearest me said, "being asked into Bahamian waters in a support. . ." His mouth closed. The ranking sailor on board was staring at him.

We cast off. The boat ran across the short distance to the cutter. It threw a pretty good wake with all of us in it.

They had to help Rolf up the ladder first. I went up next and followed the men who were taking Rolf below to be looked at by their medical officer. I could hear Chancy talking loudly to someone behind us.

I would have rather waited outside while they unwrapped my handiwork on Rolf's injured hand. But one of the men waved me inside. The medic – I doubted he was a doctor on a boat of this size – gave Rolf a shot first, a local that would not knock him all the way out. Rolf lay in one of the bunks. His hand lay on a plastic sheet. When his eyes closed the medic began unwrapping. I had seen it before; but it was uglier now.

"Can't do much with this," the medic said. "He's going to need to professional help." But he stopped any bleeding and closed the wound. The wrapping he put on it was tighter and more professional looking. He hooked up an I.V. started some blood back into Rolf.

"This man's lost a lot of blood. Whoever wrapped this did as good of a job as you can do with what you had. Probably saved his life. Still, you're lucky we came along."

"What are you doing out here?" I asked the medic.

His eyes swept to another of the two sailors in the

room. No one answered my question.

I was led to a small galley where I found Chancy leaning over a cup of coffee. His head lifted to me, and I hesitated half a step before I sat down across from him at the steel table. Red rims were around his eyes, he needed a shave, and his salty hair stuck out in many directions. I realized my appearance was no doubt patterned along similar lines, but I didn't want to seek out a mirror and check.

The medic had looked over Chancy's somewhat mottled head before he got busy on Rolf. He had told Chancy that there was not anything wrong with him that time and maybe a vacation would not fix. This had not helped Chancy's mood.

A mess sailor slipped a white ceramic mug in front of me. I was looking around the galley. Three men sat in the far corner. The other half dozen tables were unoccupied. The smell of the coffee drifted up to me. I took a sip.

"Wow," I said. "This is good coffee – no doubt made from contented beans."

Chancy was frowning, looking down at the five cigars and two dripping reels that he had placed on the table beside his cup. The reels were both golden-plated Penns. They made a stark contrast with the gray of everything around us. The walls, floors, ceiling – everything was gray or polished steel. The men who moved around us could have been made of the same stuff. No one spoke to us. They moved in some rigid sense of duty. But there was an underlying sense of excitement I had trouble placing.

"It's a good thing we weren't out after bonefish," I said. "You'd have had along those two new Billy Pate reels and your good fly rods. That would have been a couple or three thousand dollars worth of equipment right there."

"We wouldn't have been on the ocean then."

"There's that," I nodded.

"You remember to grab the camera?"

"It had been under water. I doubt it was worth saving."

"Figures."

"We have our lives, and Rolf's." Chancy was looking down into his half-filled cup. His head lifted slowly to me. He leaned closer, spoke softly, "Those fellows over there." He nodded toward the three in the corner.

I let my eyes sweep past the corner again, then looked back at Chancy. "Yeah?"

"The fellow this side took off an ATF hat earlier. The other fellows look like Navy SEALs."

"And?"

The click of heels coming into the galley cut off any response, if there was going to be one. An officer I had not seen yet came up to our table and stopped. "We'll be putting you off in a seven minutes. Is there anything. . ."

"Putting us off?" Chancy said. "You're putting us on's more like it. We can't be to Hope Town already."

"No, sir. We will be setting you down on Elbow Cay, on the ocean side. One of the boats there, or a ferry, can take you to Hope Town, or across to Marsh Harbour if your friend needs further medical attention."

"First it's the Mr. Christian who brings us on board. Now this." Chancy's face, already red, got darker. "We're U.S. citizens, and we have an injured man here. I don't seem to be . . ."

But the officer had spun and was walking away.

"Well, we will damned well find out. . ." Chancy let that hang as well.

Six minutes later Chancy and I were supporting a

groggy Rolf, helping him into the RIB. The sun was bright and we had no dark glasses. The three of us blinked like moles as we climbed in along with three of the sailors. The sea was still cutting up a bit in the wind around us, but the cutter barely moved up and down in it. The shoreline of Elbow Cay was close enough to make out the Abaco Inn and the cottages that dotted the shoreline on either side of it. A crane lifted us and we rose over the railing and were lowered to the surface where we bobbed once the cable was undone.

In the distance a black plume of smoke rose above the island. A couple of the sailors squinted in that direction. Once – in a visit a year or two back – Chancy and I had taken a wrong turn on one of the island's few roads and had found ourselves at the dump, where anything hard was buried and anything that could be burned was tossed into a smoldering fire that burned on most week days. I figured that for the source of the smoke.

The scarab cut through the bit of reef, zipping us over to the litter-scattered shore. A fellow stood on the sand waiting for us. The boat must have radioed across to let them know.

As soon as the RIB pulled up on the sand, two of the sailors hopped out and pulled us higher. The waiting fellow headed right for Rolf and helped him out of the boat. Chancy and I had barely stepped out when the sailors spun the boat and headed back toward the cutter.

"That's no frigate," Chancy said to Rolf.

Rolf turned his head slowly on his now-stooped shoulders. He looked at the Coast Guard boat. "No. Frigate's over four-hundred feet and is Navy vessel. Is about two-hundred-seventy feet, draws fourteen. Is why it couldn't take us into Hope Town. We're an hour from low tide."

I had no way of knowing how he knew about the tide, but a glance around the beach told me he was probably right.

"Extended hanger, back behind the funnel," Rolf said, "houses HH 605 Jayhawk helicopter."

"And those bastards wouldn't fly you to where you could get help?" Chancy stared out at the cutter.

"Come on," the fellow who had come to meet us said. "Let's get out of the open."

"What's going on?" Chancy said. "I'm staying here until you tell us."

"Fine with me," the fellow said. He started across a board over the sharp coral points that led up onto a path.

"For a Coast Guard boat, it's a helluva way from the coast," Chancy muttered as he followed.

Once across the razor-like coral-surrounded path that led up to the Inn, and having skirted the deserted pool, we came through the newer waist-high coconut growth, sea grape, and hibiscus. Coming out of all that green, my attention was drawn to the brown wall of sandbags piled high around the inn.

Out along the piers, where the Inn's saltwater fishing boat and any rental boats of the guests were kept, a few bows and a broken spar stuck out of the water. The piers were scorched. Broken, twisted boards stuck out at different angles.

"Looks like a war zone," I said.

"Should," the fellow said who led us.

Inside the Inn it was dark. The hurricane shutters had been battened down. Plywood panels covered what would have been open spaces in the normally open bar area. It looked like hurricane season, which does not begin here in earnest most years until September.

Half a dozen people were huddled at a couple of the

tables in the dim bar room. Empty bottles of beer were piled up in front of a couple of the men.

"Beer's warm by now, but help yourselves," our guide said. "I'm Manny Argento, the manager."

"We didn't come here for the ambiance," Chancy said.

"We need to get our friend to a doctor." I said.

"And I need to check on my wife." Chancy was looking at a shotgun someone had leaned beside the door.

"We're cut off here," Manny said. "No boats. No vehicles. You can try the radio. But most of the people are holed up together in groups. Doubt your wife stayed alone. If she's not one of. . . ."

"Anyone want to tell us what's going on?" Chancy asked. "Are we at war? It's the natives isn't it. They've risen up."

The people at the tables, four men and two women who looked as though they'd been stretched to their nerve ends, traded glances.

"No," Manny said. "Or almost no. It's not our natives – well, one or two of 'em. The trouble's from a couple of posses of Jamaicans got run in here by ATF officers. And when I say posses, I mean major ones, fifty to a hundred men in each – bad as wild dogs. They took hostages, fought a running gun fight with some of our boys. It's still goin' on. Houses were burned. Most every boat or vehicle was wrecked or stolen. Most our natives, and the Haitian camps have taken to cover themselves long as any shootin's goin' on."

"And the U.S. Navy?" Chancy said.

"Have been asked not to come onto our islands. We all know how your boys like to come in shootin' and such. But we'll handle it our ways. May take longer, but we'll still have an island or two left."

"And a doctor?" I pressed again.

"Hope Town's your bet. You might make a go of it come night. Though you're takin' your chances. But hell, you're takin' 'em bein' here. I can't guarantee you. . . ."

"We'll start now," Chancy said. "That okay with you two?"

I looked to Rolf. Tired as he was, he nodded. "Sure," I said. It was stuffy in the closed up bar, and smelled of stale beer. The looks on the faces of the folks there was not doing me a world of good either.

"Any weapons we can take?" Chancy asked.

"You're probably better off without any," Manny said. He lifted a make-shift bar that rested across the inside of the door, something that would last less than a second if anyone really wanted in. The sun beat down on us. It was a humid day, though there were no clouds. "I'll get you some water," Manny said. "Least I can do for ya." He went back inside.

"You sure about this, Chance?" I asked.

"Stay if you want."

Manny came back out into the sunlight with three liter bottles of water. I reached for Rolf's, but Rolf held out his good hand, took one of the bottles. We started to our left, up the road that led past Rudy's and to the house we had rented. Hope Town was an hour's walk beyond that.

In the distance I heard what sounded like a couple of shots. Sweat began pouring off us as soon as we started walking. Gnats and a mosquito or two whirled around us when we walked through calm stale patches of air in the lee of clumps of the trees.

Houses were strung along on either side of the road. But we did not see another person. The only sounds were the wind high in the trees and the rustle of leaves. We rounded a curve in the road. Ahead of us a small car lay on its side beside the road, blackened by a fire that had left it a gutted beetle. Smoke still rose from its smoldering upholstery.

"One of us had better go on point," Chancy said, "so we don't surprise ourselves by stumbling onto whoever's doing all this." He was looking at me.

I walked alone up the road while they waited, standing near an eight foot high clump of yellow-striped green grass, a dracaena plant – some call it a "dragon plant," others a "money tree." They could get behind it if they needed. Broken shell bits strewn across the irregular and chuck hole marked concrete of the road crunched beneath my steps. It was more quiet than it should have been. The houses I could see from the road either were boarded shut or stood with doors open. Some of the doors tilted out on broken hinges. Bits of stereo components and other possessions were scattered out into the lanes that led to the road as if each of the homes had been systematically raided. Smoke trickled out from the charred shell of one home. A fire had swept its insides. I could see through the blackened window frames on this side out through what was once the deck that faced the ocean.

I found myself walking closer to the edge of the road, ready to dart into the scrub at the slightest sound.

I wanted to tell Chancy that this was nothing like the Bahamas we came to so often – no steady chattering hum of people on their decks having a mid-day beverage, no Jimmy Buffett music wailing over it all, no locals acting half resentful while holding out hands for American dollars. All that was obvious to the eye, but I wanted to talk. I had never felt so social, wanting to speculate with Rolf about what my wife, or ex-wife perhaps by now, might be up to. I believe it was Lewis Grizzard who said, "I'm not going to marry any more. I'm just going to find a woman I hate and give her a house."

A hermit crab scuttled out across the sand at the edge of the road and carried its brown-striped whelk shell across my path. I stood like a lawn statue and watched, realized how tense I was letting myself become.

As soon as I stopped I heard the soft sound of crunching shells and the whir of wheels ahead, around the bend in the road. I whirled and waved to Chancy and Rolf to get off the road. They both shot off, slipping behind the dragon plant.

The sound I heard became clearly that of a golf cart as it neared. Much as I wanted to stand in the road, hope for friendly islanders, the thought of the burned out cottages and vehicles got my feet moving.

The woods to my left was too sparse to hide even my fireplug build. Farther ahead the vegetation along the road would become dense matted green prickly walls on either side. Here, though, a few dark boles of coconut trees, their sweeping trunks covered with hummingbird's trumpet vine, a broad-leafed banana plant or two, and a few crepe myrtle bushes were sprinkled along a slope that ran up to a house, were all there was to hide among. I glanced around, then dove to my right.

Along that side of the road a canal ran parallel, with wooden piers jutting out between cypress trees and thick clumps of mangroves. I jumped a small pile of empty gas cans and the litter of boat motor parts corroded orange by the salt. As the sound came around the corner I slipped into the shadow beneath the nearest pier, climbed up onto the criss-cross of wooden supports, and clung to the underside of the pier – hidden, I hoped.

Beneath me, sharp jutting cypress knees stuck up among open clam and mollusk shells – all covered by a drying black ooze left behind by the tide. Small crabs clambered through the damp black hills and valleys of the shoreline like devouring spiders. Within a foot of my head, where I clung, a web was spread across the wooden corner, centered by a fiddle-backed spider I thought looked a lot like a brown recluse. While I watched the spider twitch its long legs restlessly, I felt one or two splinters I had picked up in the scramble, one on the inside of my palm where I clenched the underside of the pier. The spider stirred from the center of its web and began to sidle in a deliberate manner toward my hand nearest the web. Altogether, there are many places I have been in my life I found more charming.

The golf cart moved slowly, cautiously along the road. I could hear the low mutter of voices. I had heard enough Jamaican accents to know the real thing. These were not the loud blustering voice I expected. They were the low, controlled voices of professionals. I listened while moving slowly out from the crossing braces, away from the spider. I hung by my clenched fingers, with my ankles crossed over one antique two-by-four.

High above, and from a distance, I heard the tight whop whop whop roar of an approaching helicopter. I could see tiny slices of the sky through the cracks between the boards above me, but I could not see the sky in the direction from which I placed the sound.

On the road, the cart stirred gravel as it slid to a sideways stop, then revved in a whine as the driver smashed off the road into vegetation not fifty feet from where I hung with tiring fingers.

Pounding padded feet took off in several directions from the cart. One set came in my direction. A rock clattered against the shells beneath me, knocked that way by a bare dark foot that soon followed. There was a scurry of hustling escaping crabs, the sound of wincing barefoot steps on the shells and muck below, then the heavy breathing of someone panting, looking up at the sky from the shadow of the pier.

I guess I had expected dreadlocks and the bright clothing of some Jamaican steel drum fantasy. The fit and muscular fellow below me had fairly short hair under his tight knitted cap. He wore an army green t-shirt and fatigues. He looked very business-like, held some sort of automatic weapon. He backed up until he stood directly beneath me, then he looked up and saw me.

FREEPORT, The Bahamas – All reserves of the Royal Bahamian Police force have been unexpectedly called into active duty as of 7 p.m. last evening. No official report has been released on the action, though our correspondents have lost radio contact with Exuma, Rum Cay and parts of the Abaco Islands.

Chapter Six

His eyes opened into white rings on his dark face, and his shoulders tilted back. He began to lift the automatic weapon, in slow motion it seemed to me, one finger sliding forward to click off the safety. The click seemed very loud to my heightened senses. The helicopter passed overhead. Its hard chopping began to fade into a dim roar in the distance. From down the road I heard a shouted, "Come out dahr wit you!"

The spider had been creeping along the board above me, following my movement as I sought to ease away. It suddenly shot across the wood, ran across the back of my aching hand and darted up my forearm. I let go with my hands and ankles and fell.

My back hit first, banging against something hard, the rifle or his head. The rest of him I hit was softer. It broke my fall before I landed in a tangle and rolled. I felt the muck and nick of razor-edged shells on my forearms. I scrambled to my feet. He lay still. His neck was bent at an angle, and one of the cypress knees stuck up out of his chest like a small bloody spear. I gasped, took a step back.

The gun lay there. I grabbed it and crawled out from the shadow into the bright sunlight. Two men in similar uniform were pointing guns at the dragon tree. Rolf and Chancy were stepping out from behind it. Their hands were up. I was too far to see a clear expression on their faces.

The gun I held, when I gave it a closer glance, was an AK-47. I had heard of automatic weapons like this before, but had never handled one. Now was not the time to dwell on that. This one looked like a big ten-pound pistol with a banana clip and an extendable stock. I found the selective fire switch on the right side of the receiver. It had three clicks. Up was for safety. It was set on the middle click now, which could be either semi-automatic or fully automatic.

I eased up onto the edge of the road, keeping my feet on what vegetation I could find as I moved closer. Twenty feet away, the Jamaican closest to me turned his head and spotted me. He spun, glared, and started to lift his weapon. It looked to be a short uzi. His hands were squeezing and I lifted to his eyes, saw only earnest intent there.

The shots blasted the still, hot air. His look of intent changed to shock. He tried to look down at himself, jerked back instead when the second round hit him. I was as surprised as he was that I had squeezed the trigger. I felt the gun jerking in my hands where I held the gun down at my hip in an unprofessional manner.

The other fellow spun. I couldn't tell if he was going to shoot or run. But I turned to him and squeezed off a short flurry of rounds that lifted him into the air and dropped him.

"Holy tam Rambo," Rolf said. He moved closer to look down at the two dead men.

All this happened in a very few seconds, shocked ones for me. I blinked, saw the men laying there. Chancy and Rolf grabbed one of the men by the ankles and dragged him toward the bush. The dragged body left a red thin line from the edge of the road that was soon lost in the plant life. They headed back for the other one, "Get their clips too," Chancy said. I blinked again, realized I was standing in the same spot.

I turned and forced myself back to the pier, ducked

back under into the shadows. The man there was just as dead as I had left him. I reached for him, but could not bring myself to go through his pockets. I undid a military belt with pouches he wore and tugged that loose. It jostled him as the belt and pouches passed under him. I held the gun and belt, looked down at him longer than I should have. All of it suddenly had some impact on me. I took a step or two and retched, dry hard retches from not eating.

"What's taking so long?" Chancy called to me in a shouted whisper.

I staggered over to the edge of the water, cupped a handful of saltwater and scrubbed my face with it. My face felt puffy and unreal, like Chancy's had looked earlier after the swelling had gone down. I felt more of the nausea, but could not retch any more. I avoided looking at the body as I crawled back out.

Chancy and Rolf both held guns. Chancy's shirt pockets bulged with clips. Rolf had picked up a small khaki day pack and had slipped his water bottle in that so he could carry a weapon. "We'd better not try to go by cart," Chancy said. "Being on foot'll give us a chance to react or hide if we have to."

Both of them were looking at me. I did not have anything I wanted or needed to say. The looks they gave me had surprised admiration in them. It made me feel almost as swell as looking at the bodies had. I turned and nodded to the sparse woods to our left, began to walk that direction.

"Lead on, Natty Bumpo," Chancy said.

"By geez-tam. He's one Annie-tam-Oakley. Saved our bacons."

"Better hope the goat world never hears he rescued you," Chancy said. He was whispering now as we entered the shadows of the trees and started to move beside the road.

We had barely gone a quarter of a mile before the growth began to close up on us.

"Where you going, Davy Crockett?" Chancy said when I veered left.

"There's a path that runs behind the houses. Might be better for us to take it than walk down the middle of the road.

As if in confirmation, the sound of wheels and a gas engine came in a rush down the road in our direction. We ducked behind a thick stand of croton, with its brilliant red, yellow, and green thick leaves, and a Frangipani plant. I moved aside a yellow and white bloom and a few of the wide green leaves of the Frangipani and saw the dark faces, the weapons, the wide knitted caps of half a dozen wildly dressed blacks in a small white pickup. All of these men seemed to have the dreadlock hair style.

"Thought the Rastas had wrecked all the vehicles," Chancy whispered.

"Not the ones they use," Rolf suggested.

As soon as the vehicle was past, I rose and led us up past the back of a tightly sealed rock home into a grove of lime, orange, and grapefruit trees.

"You find these back trails peeking into homes at night, or what?" Chancy said.

I didn't answer.

Chancy grabbed a half-ripe orange from a tree. I picked up three ripe star fruits from the ground beneath a tree at the edge of the grove.

"Those good to eat?" Rolf asked.

"Sorry," I said, realizing that his good hand was filled carrying a gun. I slipped the fruits into his pack, picked a couple more of the riper ones off the tree for myself.

At the back of the grove a path opened leading into the

woods. Turning to our right took us in a somewhat parallel direction to the road.

"Watch for this stuff." I pointed out a tree that leaned out into our path. Its leaves came in groups of five, each shiny and green. The trunk of the tree was gray, mottled with black patches where the sap had oozed through and stained the bark. "It's poisonwood. You get next to it and you'll think poison ivy is for amateurs."

"Any of this other stuff poison?" Rolf waved to another plant at the back of the garden.

"That's a night-blooming cereus," I said. "We'd better get moving if you don't want to be here to see it bloom."

"He knows the names of quite a few things," Chancy said, "but not much regarding their inner workings."

I let that hang in the air for a moment without responding.

"Okay to smoke here?" Chancy said. He had one of his cigars out and was lighting it before I could reply. It took a second to sink in that he had asked my permission.

I walked up front as we followed the trail. It was mostly beaten down dirt, here and there packed gravel. A root sometimes stuck out of the dirt and slanted across the path. But it was light enough, even in the shade of the trees, to see each snag and trip.

Several times we heard helicopters buzz past overhead. We stayed tight to the densest cover when we heard them coming. We knew too little about what was going on.

We had one tight spot where we had to dash across a road and walk in the open for a quarter of a mile. The growth was too thick along either side of the road for us to move through. The engine of another vehicle coming up the road was heading toward us when we got to the small fork in the road and dodged off into the path that led toward our rented house. We hurried deep into cover before the vehicle went past.

The late afternoon sun had baked the moisture from the tropical wood's dark floor. A gray lizard raced across the trail ahead of us, made more noise with its crackling of leaves than we were making.

We left the path and went along a narrow cement walk that led around a boarded-up house that neighbored our rental. We followed the path down until it led past a tool shed and the harbor inlet where we docked our boat. The pier looked lonely and empty now. I had not thought for a while of our boat and stuff out bobbing in the waves and slowly filling with water.

A walk of small flagstones, flat pieces of limestone and coral all cemented together, led up to our house. I was not halfway up the path when I sensed something very wrong. The doors all stood open wide. A piece of what could be a broken length of expensive fly rod lay among the shattered debris I had to step over.

"What . . .?" Chancy shot around me and ran toward the house. A few feet from the door, and still running, he called out, "Myrna?"

Rolf bumped into me. I realized I had stopped. I did not expect a reply from Myrna.

"Does not look good, eh?" Rolf said. He did not look so swell himself. Veins showed thin and red beneath cheeks that seemed less round and nearly transparent and pale. His eyes were rummy-wet and red.

"No."

We climbed the stairs to the main floor. My stuff was, or had been, in a room on the ground floor. I was in no hurry to see what that room looked like.

Chancy came out of the master bedroom. He still clutched the uzi. His eyes were wide, his brow tightened into ripples.

All the cabinets had been opened. What had not been worth taking had been tumbled out onto the floor or smashed against the walls.

"They wrecked all the rods and reels," Chancy said. "The Scott, the Winston, my favorite Thomas & Thomas. They smashed the Billy Pate reels with a hammer. Didn't want the fly fishing gear. Just destroyed it all to be doing something."

"Myrna?" I said.

"Gone," he said. "No sign of her."

"That could be good," I said. "Maybe she. . ."

He gave a start. "Something for you by the frig." He rushed out the open door that led out onto the upper back deck. He was out there only a second or two, came back through and was thumping down the front stairs.

Rolf stood just inside the door, the way one will when half-invited. He looked as comfortable as someone who had walked into the middle of a domestic dispute. He stirred and went over toward the open refrigerator, pointed to something stuck to the wall. "This for you?"

I went over to look at the yellow piece of paper. It was a telegram that had come for me. Someone had opened it and stuck it to the wall with a now-bent paring knife. It said, "You're a bachelor again, you son-of-a-bachelor. Dorothy." It was from Las Vegas.

"Nice of her to take time to write," Rolf said.

"This day needed that," was all I could manage.

We come down here for no phones, television, connection with the world, and some S.O.B. manages to get a telegram through to me. A well-intentioned, kind soul, the agent who rented us the house perhaps, must have dropped it by earlier.

"What now?" Rolf said.

"Find you a doctor." He had been a quiet trooper. But

I had seen him wince a time or two on the hike. He was a different fellow from the round, pinkish and hale Rolf I had first met.

We went down the stairs. Chancy stood staring out across the garden path that led down to the pier. I gave him a moment or two, went to pay a belated visit to the room where everything I had brought was broken, stolen, or ripped to bits. Whoever had done all this had taken time to be thorough in leaving a message.

When we stay in the Bahamas we never lock the doors of the place we rent. No local would dare enter a home. Crime of that sort out on the far islands is simply not a factor. Like Chancy, I had left my passport and a few hundred dollars in cash in my room. All of it was gone. I had even lost a cache of Power Bars, which in the nature of these events hit me harder than it should have. There was nothing left in the house to eat. We had only the water bottles we carried. Everything else had been taken. The tap water at these rental homes comes from cisterns where rain water is collected, and where small frogs breed in happy squalor. I had tried drinking the local water before and had been sorry. It was a good way to get a dysentery that could spoil any trip. The locals were used to it. But a tender tourist could get surprised by the water in ice cubes or even that used to wash vegetables for a salad. If it came to that, we could drink the local water, but in the end might risk dehydration from doing it.

I went back out to the front of the house where Chancy was looking straight ahead at nothing and talking in a monotone to Rolf, who shrugged at me.

". . .trailer homes being flattened by hurricanes, the housing of the poor being flooded by rivers because the homes were built too close to a flood plane," Chancy was saying," is something we get used to. But when those fires swept the Monterey area, wiped out some homes of really wealthy people, or those earthquakes that. . ."

"Chancy," I said. "Chancy."

He stopped and turned to stare at me. "Hope Town?" I said.

He blinked, seemed on the verge of rejoining us when the sound of the bullet hitting the house behind us snapped us all fully awake. Rolf clubbed Chancy with his good hand, knocking him to the ground. I dove beside them, jarred the ground hard with my forearms, rolled to my left, hearing the crack of more shots now.

"Hey, Dot. How long you been down here at the tables? Didn't you hear the news?"

"What news?"

"The CNN guy says something's going on out there in the Bahamas. "You're lucky you didn't. . ."

"What kind of something?"

"Hard to tell. He mentioned half the islands. I thought he said Abaco."

"My luck the bastard's already changed his insurance."

Chapter Seven

I wriggled forward until I was up against the bole of a buttercup tree with a low stand of croton beside it. Chancy and Rolf were scrambling for better cover to my right. The house was behind us. A shot ricochetted off the walk, took out one of the small lights that line the path and make finding the house at night easier, when there is power.

The gun I held felt hot to my touch though I had not fired it. I clasped it tighter than I needed to and peeked around the tree. Two wheelbarrows sat beside the door of the house to the left of ours, the one we had passed on our way here. The men had started to pry at the boards, they had not gotten the house open yet. A man in a huge drooping multi-colored knit beret was standing by the door. His gun bucked and I heard the shot take out a window behind me. It was some pretty lousy shooting.

I didn't want to fire back, had promised myself I would do everything I could not to shoot anyone else if I could help it.

A shot came from our far right. The man to my left flew back, bounced off the outside wall of the house, and fell. Another black face popped around the corner of the house, looked down at him and then in our direction. It was not the face of someone who expected to be shot back at. Another fellow stood holding the handles of a wheelbarrow. A burst of shots came from the trees to our right. The face at the corner of the building zipped out of sight. The fellow holding the wheelbarrow let go and dove to the concrete path. He rolled from there across garden mulch until he was behind a low row of bushes. Shots ripped through the leaves and thudded into the house behind him.

I could see the fellows to the right now, three blacks dressed as the first few we had met. The two men by the house began to shoot back at them. Bits of bark flew off a tree beside one of them who dashed behind the wide trunk just in time. I had no idea how long this was going to go on. It looked like it was settling into being an all day affair. I caught movement to my right. Chancy stood up from behind his bush. He held a gun in each hand. He sprayed the men to the right first, then spun and sent some rounds toward the men huddled by the house. I don't believe he came within a foot of any of them. But they looked our way and saw him. I was standing now too. In ones and twos they scrabbled from their spots and took off running in the directions from which they had come.

I moved closer to Chancy, still keeping my eye on the area of the small firefight. He was breathing hard and staring that way too.

"Must've thought we were Royal Bahamas Police Force," he said. I moved the rest of the way to him. Maybe I expected him to look a little cocky. But he looked surprised, a little worried. I looked down. Rolf lay in a tuck, the side of his face pressed against the gravel under a bush. His skin was as pale as I'd seen it. I could not detect his breathing.

"Is he. . . ?"

"No," Chancy said. "But he's out. How do you feel about lugging your pal around through the jungle. He's got to be two-fifty at least."

I bent down, felt Rolf's pulse – faint, but there. "We can't leave him here."

"Good luck carrying him."

I stood, looked around, headed toward the neighbor's house.

"Where you going?"

"Get one of those wheelbarrows. Unless you want to carry Rolf."

The two of us struggled through half a dozen tries before we succeeded in lifting him into the wheelbarrow. As it was, his head lolled at the front and his legs were propped up at the handles. I put his pack, my water, and the guns in with him. I lifted, felt my knees pop and my spine tighten. But I was able to start up the slight slope of the path with him. Chancy carried his gun and moved into the lead.

It had been getting darker, was quite a bit darker once we entered the dense shadows of the tropical woods. There was something unfathomable, sinister, and oppressive about the way night came over the islands where there were no lights. It was like some damp burr-infested cloak scraping into place. A bird was making a clacking, gulping sound. Roaches, scorpions stirred among the harsh leaves on the ground. Wind from the sea breezes rustled high in the tree tops. Otherwise it was still as death in the woods, and getting almost as dark.

Our steps were silent. The wheel rolled smoothly, except for an occasional thump over a root or across a hole. We had no flashlights to help us see the trail.

Every now and then we could hear the sound of a distant motor of some vehicle passing on the road. An occasional shot, or burst of shots came from farther away.

I had never taken the trail all the way to Hope Town. We had always come out and walked on the road. This time we veered and stayed on the right fork of the trail that went past dark houses. The trail wove down along the water. We circled around the edge of coves, saw a house boat as dark as any of the houses. I saw light only once. We went past a small shanty with a piece of paisley cloth hung over the open door. A flicker of a candle or some other small light went out as we neared.

We passed a concrete boat ramp that led down into the dark water. The thick brush surrounding the trail opened for a stretch. The sky was as dark as it gets. I heard a scrap of music being carried across the water from some unseen source.

"Gonna be a rev-o-lut-ion, yah.
Da Natty Dread gonna be wit you."

The tinny thump of drums faded as we went back into the thicker brush.

A couple of times we came out of the thick brush and could see across the water and were not where we had expected to be. The first time we were in a cove, the second by a yacht basin, but not the one at Hope Town. Half a dozen fast looking boats rocked at their moorings.

We stopped to rest. Each of my arms felt an inch or two longer. I came close to leaning and resting against a poisonwood tree. But dark as it was, I saw the mottled bark in time. A firecracker string of shots went off in the distance. The boom of single answering shots followed. The trees were too thick where we stood to see the stars. The dark was wrapping tighter around us, like a damp gym sock.

"What do you make of all this?" Chancy asked. He lit one of his remaining cigars. His face looked drawn and bony in the brief flicker from his lighter. I imagine I looked as haggard.

"Just what we heard from Manny," I said, "that two large groups of Jamaicans got run onto the islands by some of our ATF people. The Jamaicans seem to be fighting among themselves and with the Bahamian police."

The cigar end went up and down in a nod. "I understand the looting. But what happened to everyone?"

"You have me there," I said. I reached for the handles and lifted Rolf. So far he had not stirred. I checked his pulse each time we stopped. His heartbeat was not keeping up with the occasional scraps of Reggae music we heard.

We came down another wrong trail, went between two cottages, and could finally see Hope Town. We were still a distance from it, on the other side of the harbor. But we could see the flames. The music was louder. So were the shots. A helicopter hung over what would be downtown Hope Town, a snug community of about two hundred natives and however many tourists. Now its only lights were the fires and the searchlight from the copter. The beam swept the houses. A door-gunner traded shots with someone on the ground. We weren't as close as we had hoped to be. But it did not look like someplace where we wanted to go. I felt a sinking defeated feeling as I lowered the wheelbarrow handles and stared across the water.

Where there should have been fifty or so yachts bobbing at their moorings, there was open water with a few mast tops sticking out of the water.

"Now what?" Chancy said.

All the energy I had been squeezing from every bit of myself ebbed away, seemed to flow down my legs and out at my socks. I felt tired, deathly tired. I wanted to lay down where I stood, curl up on the dirt and leaves, and take a nap. I even resented Rolf, laying there in the barrow, getting his rest, or dying.

"Now what?" Chancy repeated.

I heard the smallest of noises, lighter than the lizard sound earlier. I looked to the path behind us, expecting to see some snake, or a scorpion, perhaps the barrels of guns pointed at us. Instead, I saw two brown feet, wide-splayed

and worn – ones that had been bare all their owner's life.
"Chance."
"What?"
My eyes panned up thin brown legs to swollen knots of knees, tattered shorts, a once-white t-shirt worn spider web thin, to a small grinning face.
"You fellas lost? Where you wanna be?"
The second he began to speak Chancy whirled and lifted his uzi. I whipped out a hand, held the barrel, pressed it back down. "He's not one of them," I said.
"John," the man said. "I'm John." His eyes widened when he heard the safety of Chancy's gun click. I held the short barrel, kept it from lifting any higher.
"Where is everyone?" I asked.
"Most folk took off. Big fightin' goin' on over thar." He nodded toward the town.
"Just tell us. . . ."
I held up a hand to stop Chancy.
"You know where any of the others are?" I asked.
He nodded slowly, watching Chancy.
"Can you take us there?" I slid my free hand into my pocket, fumbled with the few soggy bills there. I worked loose two or three bills, could not make out in the dim light what Bahamian denomination they were. When I looked back up at John he was shaking his head.
"You folla," he said. He turned and started back on the trail.
I felt the tension ease from the gun barrel I clenched. Chancy lowered the gun, put it in with Rolf and the other weapons. I went to reach for the wheelbarrow handles, my arms still feeling stretched and my hands burning from the blisters I expected. Chancy nudged me to the side. "Give it a rest," he said. He bent and picked up the handles.
If ever I must look back to a single defining moment

by which I would like to remember Chancy, it was then. No word or deed could have been greater. I did not dwell on it. I hurried up the trail after John, feeling vigor, hope, the usual array of misguided emotions when relieved of a burden.

Behind me I heard the quiet roll and occasional bump of the wheel.

Even though I had my night eyes now, I still tripped on a root or rut now and again. I heard a soft curse from Chancy that told me his vision was no better than mine.

Barefoot John, though, made not a single misstep as he led us back the way we'd come, then off onto a divergent path that led into the thickest, densest woods we had been in yet. There were no houses for a long stretch. The brush grew in a tight living wall on either side of us. Even though the night got later, and the woods darker, it was no cooler here deep in the forest. It was humid. The trail we were on was little used. We had to step over the spikes of small plants that sought to grow up and obscure the trail altogether.

I thought about the bare feet picking their way ahead of me. Their calloused soles could well be thicker than that of the deck shoes I wore.

Around us, in the dark, came the sound of birds, and perhaps other night creatures. I thought I could make out the caw of the native Bahama parrot. But the other sounds were part of the dark mystery. Coming from somewhere ahead of us I sensed at first, then began to hear a growing hum. I wrestled with my exhausted and overwhelmed senses, eliminated a waterfall, the rush of wind, music of some soft thumping kind. John went out of sight around a curve ahead of me in the trail. I made the turn myself and found John standing still in front of the gate of a chain-link fence. The fence was a good fourteen feet high with coiled razor-edged barbed wire along its slanted top.

The wheel banged into the calf of my leg. Chancy lowered the handles and may have reached for one of the guns. I had just recognized the sound I'd been hearing as that of a generator.

Hand-held lights snapped on and the beams locked on our faces. I heard the slides being worked, could make out the barrel or two of weapons pointing at us through the fence.

"Keep your hands where we can see them. You!"

Behind me, Chancy straightened.

John stood staring ahead. Like some devoted Judas, I thought.

I was so tired it didn't matter. The one thing I fixed on, as I stood on wavering legs, waiting, was that the voice behind the gun was not Jamaican.

"Gon-na be a rev-o-lut-ion, yah."

Chapter Eight

The gate creaked open and the lights swung away from our eyes. But we stood blinking while four men in combinations of camouflage and khaki fatigues circled us and moved closer to look at our guns and Rolf in the barrow. They waved with their barrels for Chancy to put his gun in the barrow. He did.

Their white faces were firm and disinterested. "What'cha got here, John?" one of them asked.

"White fellas wanderin' 'round loose."

"This one's not in such hot shape. He shot?"

"Don' know, Mistah Malone. May be Doc Jocelyn can. . .?"

"Let's all go inside," Malone said.

Chancy and I walked behind John. One of them took over the wheelbarrow, one with a gun followed us, the other stayed behind at the gate. Malone walked between us and Rolf.

The trail turned and widened as we got closer to the hum of the generator. Above the flicker of the hand-held lights of our escort, I began to see something through the trees I had not seen for a while. Lights!

First they flickered in a yellow glow through the trees. As we got closer to the first building, small lights lined the path. Our guard, or escort, turned off their lights. No one pointed guns at us, but they held them, and we had none.

"Better take him in to see Doc," Malone said. We stood outside a low warehouse-shaped building.

"Mistah Randall. . . ?" John started to say.

"Will see them later." Malone nodded to us. "Stay put." To one of the men he said, "Take him in, Sidney."

Sidney lifted the wheelbarrow handles and John got the door. They rolled inside.

Ten minutes later John brought the barrow back out. It was empty. Sidney came out and waved Chancy and I inside with his gun.

Cool conditioned air washed over us. Instead of refreshing me, it made me feel so light and good I wanted to lay down and sleep.

The lights inside the building were not bright – forty-watt bulbs hung from cords at twenty-foot intervals. Wooden crates, boxes, cages, piles of them lined the path through which we wove. I thought I saw something move behind the open slats of one of the wooden crates. The warehouse smelled musty.

At the far wall we were led through a door. Sidney didn't follow. The lights inside were bright. Rolf lay on a high table in the center of the room. A woman in a white jacket was bent over a microscope at a desk along the wall. Shelves filled with books lined the wall. They were not medical or reference books for the most part, but novels, books of poetry. The walls, shelves, desk were all of a matching dark knotty pine. The other woman stood beside Rolf and rubbed at his face with a damp cloth. I knew her.

"Monique?" I said.

"You fellas sure been through it, eh?" She looked up and grinned. What got Rolf? Barracuda?"

I nodded, still too stunned to speak.

"Who's. . .?" Chancy managed, nodding toward the woman in the white coat. She was ignoring us.

"That's Dr. Jocelyn. Oh, that's just what folks call her. Some people new to the islands call her 'Dr. J.' But only once, and I recommend you against trying it."

The doctor looked up from her microscope and stared at us. She had an angular tanned face, long dark hair flecked with streaks of white. Her eyes were very large, the irises the color of polished steel. She seemed alert, intelligent, but only going so far with us. "Either of you A-positive?" she asked.

I shook my head. I looked to Chancy. He was nodding, had the look of a fellow ready to roll up his sleeve with a resigned motion if he had not been in short sleeves. He stepped forward.

* * *

I woke up. My back was stiff where it pressed the floor. I don't know if I woke myself up with a snore, or if it was because of some noise from Rolf. I blinked around the darkened room. A single lamp was lit in the corner where Monique tilted back against the wall in a straight wooden chair reading. She lowered the book, kept a finger in her place, and moved closer to look down at Rolf. Satisfied, she eased quietly back to her chair.

I lifted an arm and looked at my watch. It was 4 a.m. Some of the evening came back to me as I blinked and looked around the room. Monique fixing up a bullion cube in hot water each for Chancy and me – it had been the best thing I had ever tasted in my life. Dr. Jocelyn muttering as she worked on Rolf's hand. The wall of books, the wooden, still, tone of the room, the wonder I had felt at being in a lit and air conditioned room again.

"How're you doing?" Monique whispered. My head rolled her way, and found her bent forward looking down at me. I had never looked at her face this close before. Her hair was blond and straight, her eyes brown, very brown and framed by smooth skin nearly as brown. She had a small dark mole high on her right cheekbone that in no way marred her. Her teeth were bright, straight and white, her lips full and kissable. She wore a denim short-sleeved shirt open at the top three buttons. My eyes scrolled down, noticed she had no tan lines. She sat up, a hand lifting to close a shirt button. Her mouth pursed into a half frown, but she laughed it away.

"You seem healthy enough," she said. "How long were you guys out there? Since you ate at the restaurant?"

I nodded, looked over to the center table. Chancy was stretched out on a cot that had been placed parallel to Rolf's operating table. A tube ran from his arm to Rolf. I could make out nothing running through it.

I panned to Monique's face. It still contained some of the self-absorbed confidence I had recognized earlier. But it bothered me less now.

The way she was looking at me made me want to sit up, not lay there like a flipped turtle. I was aware that I had not bathed or changed, that my mouth probably smelled like the bottom side of a rock. I pushed at the floor and struggled toward a sitting position, a touch irritated when Monique had to reach over and help me sit up. I felt very weak.

"You have a better idea than I do about what we are in the middle of?" I whispered.

"You don't have to end on no preposition for my sake," she whispered back, "I can speak as good as you, should I want." She chuckled at the look on my face. "Oh, lighten up." She gave my shoulder a soft push.

"I've lost a lot in a short while," I said. "Sorry not to rollick more."

"My place, it's gone. Dr. Jocelyn's home, office, all her pets, gone. Fires and bullets. We've done all been through it. It didn't happen just only to you. And it happened to us right where we live."

When I didn't speak, she said, "Sorry to bust your chops just a bit. But you shouldn't feel pregnant."

"How did you come to be out here?" I said when I could manage a few words. "I mean with Dr. J. at this place?"

"We call her Dr. Jocelyn," Monique reminded me. "She lives in town and lets me go her rounds with her sometimes. Maybe I'd like to study medicine one day, do some good as a nurse, might could be a doctor like her."

"She's the island's doctor?"

"There're a couple of doctors. But I don't know how they came out of all the confusion. Dr. Jocelyn's a vet. That why she comes out this way."

"But she worked on Rolf?"

"People, animals. There ain't so much difference as you'd think. 'Sides, most of her practice out here is with people anyways, one way or another."

Monique still clutched the book she'd carried over.

"What were you reading?" I whispered.

She turned and sat beside me, her back to the wall behind us. She held up the book, brown cloth with yellowed pages, *A Treasury of the Familiar*. "Makes me feel better reading over stuff I heard as a kid," she said, "when I ain't got nothin' else left now."

My lip may have curled for a second when I saw the book. I stopped it and was sorry for doing it.

"I was reading over about 'Abdul A-BulBul A-Mir,'" she said, "and 'The Shooting of Dan McGrew.' Silly stuff, but it reminds me of my poppa readin' to me as a kid, of bein' cozy in a house, back before I had to go and live somewhere else."

I felt low enough without saying anything about that.

"Listen at this one," she said, opening the book where

she held it. Her eye ran down to one of the stanzas in the poem in front of her. She read,

> *I want to give some measure running o'er,*
> *And into angry hearts I want to pour*
> *The answer soft that turneth wrath away;*
> *I'm sure I shall not pass again this way.*

"See what I mean?" She closed the book and looked at me. "You're awful hungry, ain't you?"

They had been pouring water and soup into us since we had arrived. I don't think the gnawing she saw in my face was food hunger. "I could stand a visit to the boy's room," I said.

She helped me to my feet. I resented it less this time. Rolf and Chancy still slept. Monique looked at each of them. She went back to her chair by the light, opening her book as she sat down.

I was surprised to find the door to the room unlocked. The warehouse room outside was still lit by its row of bulbs, the air still cooled by the throbbing generator's power. Conditions were stable in the room. Air conditioning a warehouse this big seemed like a lot of bother. I bent close to one of the wooden crates that had air-spaced slats. I saw the golden-orange scales along the side of a python. In another box I saw dozens of box tortoises. These were all cold-blooded animals. The cool air kept them sedated, but healthy.

"I wouldn't get too close to some of those," a voice whispered. I panned right, saw Jocelyn's face sticking out of a blanket, her eyes barely open. Her cot was back between some cages and the wall, out here in the quiet away from the rest of us.

I gave a small wave and hurried on. The door outside

was also unlocked. I had entertained the idea that we were some sort of prisoners. But that had been off.

A man rose up from a lounge chair propped against the outside of the building. It was Sidney. He held an automatic weapon. A drooping cigarette glowed in his face. He caught my look, nodded. "The bushes over there," he said.

Seeing the gun, and the man spring up like that had reminded me of the dream that had awakened me. I kept seeing the dead Jamaican under the pier, again and again. I could imagine the crabs having a go at him after the tide had its turn. None of it was pretty, nor anything to be proud of. While I was out there, I was abruptly sick again.

Back inside, I hurried to the room, careful to make as little noise as possible for the sleeping doctor. Monique handed me a cup of bullion. "Sorry. It's all we got for right now."

Chancy stirred, but didn't wake. It was so quiet in the room I could hear Rolf and Chancy's breathing.

We stood close, the steaming cup held between us. Over its rim, as I sipped, I watched her face. She was as patient and full of native goodness as some Madonna. This mess was bringing out the best in her. That, or I had never noticed much about her before.

"When I travel," I whispered, "I like to feel a touch of the surreal, to know I'm someplace far away where the rules are different and the challenges not like the daily stress I wrestle with back there. I've come to crave that sense a bit. But I never expected anything like this."

"The important thing to remember," she whispered back, her brown eyes unblinking in the smooth tanned skin of her face, "is that it's not just happening to you."

"Yeah, but. . ."

"And that every kinda person has stress. Every mail

clerk, store flunkie, boat hand, every. . ."

"Waitress?"

"You got a problem with that?"

"Absolutely not."

"You say it, but you think I couldn't never mix in your circles."

"You're doing it right now."

"Some circle."

"Yeah. Some circle."

She was out of things to say. Her eyes swept the room, checked on the patient.

"How's Rolf?" I whispered.

"He's one tough nut. He'll be fine. We've done had fellas hurt worse'n that by fish. Besides, most sailors his age can take it. If the rum hasn't pickled them, the saltwater has."

"You were going to tell me about what's going on," I said. I was more aware than I should have been of how close we were pressed together to whisper.

"You were asking. That don't mean I was telling." She chuckled softly to herself at my expression. "Oh, unknot your shorts. I was just a pulling at you."

I took a sip from the mug, burned my lip and tongue in the process.

"There's Johnny Be Bad and Red Dreadman. They lead two of the baddest posses in all Jamaica. From what we can make out, Johnny Be Bad's posse was heading back down through the islands after picking up a load of automatic weapons up in Florida someplace. What they didn't know was that Red Dreadman's bunch was waiting for them. Red's bunch come swoopin' in on Johnny's boats while they were still at sea, trying to bushwack 'em and take the guns. But what neither group knew was that some of your country's ATF men were tracking Johnny, following him down this way to see what becomes of the guns. Well, first there was the fight between the two Jamaican posses. But it'd barely got started when here comes a cutter and a couple of patrol boats with the ATF on board. All the Jamaican boats split up and went every direction there is. Most of them, though, got run right to ground here in the Bahamas on one island or another. Then they started giving us all kinds of hell. Doc Jocelyn and I was following the whole thing on the radio. You gotta remember that the Bahamas is made up of seven hundred islands. Those Jamaicans were everywhere at once. We heard of big doings at Exuma, some of the other places. Next thing we knew we were in the middle of our own mess. Soon as they were on land, the trouble hit when the two posses set to fighting with each other. Maybe if they hadn't of they'd have been too much for the few police we had coming at them. They been looting and burning all over the island, each batch of 'em having to support the hostages they took as well as their selves."

"So that's what we're up against," I said.

I heard the door close quietly, then Jocelyn's voice. "There's some who think the real villain in all this is the United States."

Island - Russ Hall

*". . .into angry hearts I want to pour
the answer soft that turneth wrath away. . ."*

Chapter Nine

"You're talking rot." The voice came from Chancy's cot. He was half sitting up, with his weight on his elbows.

"Wot. Wot." Rolf said. His eyes were blinking. He struggled to wake.

"Isn't she?" Chancy looked at me.

I shrugged. "I haven't heard what she has to say yet. I don't know."

I liked the way the steel of her eyes flashed, though. She was a serious-looking woman. But, I suspected that under different circumstances she could laugh. I don't know all I should about the chemistry of individuals, what makes some fall in love, others not. But to her Chancy was flint. Her eyes never left his, never flinched. She didn't seem the type to back off.

"Rot," Chancy said again. "Absolute rot."

Jocelyn was almost a head taller than Monique. I hadn't picked up on that earlier. They could well be mother and daughter, but acted more like sisters.

The doctor walked across the room, ignoring Chancy. She poured water into the pot, then put it back on the hotplate to heat up.

When she turned back to us, leaning back against the counter she spoke to me. "The first thing you learn when treating fire ant colonies is that when you spray them they shift to a defensive posture, generate new queens and head out in all directions. If you're not careful, you can compound your problem, not solve it."

"I thought we were talking about the ATF here." Chancy said.

"If you know what I'm going to say before I say it, go ahead," Jocelyn told him.

When he didn't respond, she continued. "Back in the '80s the Columbian drug routes were through the Caribbean into Florida. The Bush, Sr. and Reagan administrations turned up the heat here, so the routes shifted through Mexico in the early '90s."

"That's still DEA, not ATF, "Chancy said.

Jocelyn's head turned to him, slowly, and fixed him with a stare that would have melted the steel sides off that cutter on which we had been guests. Then she went on speaking. "San Diego, Texas, and Arizona all were on the pipeline map for a while. The Narcs focused on that and slowed those routes down. But, traffic is traffic. The routes have shifted back to this sector. Your DEA will never have enough money to shut off all routes forever as long as they're working with millions against outfits working in billions of dollars."

"That's obvious," Chancy said. He looked at the tube in his arm. "Hey. How much of me are you giving him?"

"None right now. It's turned off," Jocelyn said. "We left it open in case we needed it, and because you dozed off and we didn't want to wake you. Go ahead and take it out, Monique. The patient seems to be doing fine."

Rolf's eyes were open, but he lay still, listening to us. His eyes were roaming the room.

Jocelyn poured steaming water over a tea bag and continued talking. Without the white coat of the night before, she wore khaki shorts and an olive M*A*S*H t-shirt. She was trim and fit, but not without the required degree of curves to add interest to her semi-snug clothes. "Just this year the U.S. government has been pressuring the Jamaican government for an agreement that would allow U.S. Coast Guard and Navy vessels to penetrate

Jamaica's 12-mile international limit when in pursuit of vessels they believe to be carrying drugs. Other Caribbean countries, including ours, have already made that kind of agreement."

"Okay, what's the punch line," Chancy said. "Why didn't the Jamaican government go for it?"

"Actually, the Jamaican government had no problems with it, as long as the United State agreed to operate on terms set by the Jamaican government when in those waters. What they got instead was strong-arm tactics saying that Jamaica would be 'decertified' for American economic aid if they didn't comply with the U.S. version of the terms."

"As one of the taxpaying contributors to that kind of aid, I say jolly good." He sat up, rubbed the spot where the needle had been. "You think I could get some tea?"

"Pot's on the ring," Jocelyn said. He stood, tottered for half a step before crossing to the pot. She said, "You seem to favor the perspective of controlling others in their countries better than you might if it was your own country. You realize you Americans use money like a club."

"We walk softly and carry a big one, though," Chancy said.

"There's nothing soft about the way your country is walking," she said. "I must say it's rallied most of the islands against the States. No one can recall when relations have been as frosty." She unlocked from the eye duel they were having and looked at me. "First it's the drugs, then it's the weapons. The same with the DEA, and now, the ATF. The drug traffickeres did get all the ink, making it easy for a while to ship weapons south from Florida through the islands. The gun-running down here rose to an all time high. The number of homicides in Jamaica, nine hundred last year, was as high as that of New York City, which has three times as many people."

"The ratio of Bahamian homicides sure must be having a boom this week," Chancy said. "I can't see how anything you've said has an iota to do with what we're going through here."

"The point is, that now the ATF is riding on the same heavy-handed tactics policies of your government. I don't say what they're trying to do is wrong, just the way they're going about it."

"You some kind of arm-chair coach about enforcement agencies?" Chancy asked.

Jocelyn let out a hard exasperated puff of breath. Her lips pressed together. She glanced at Monique, then back to Chancy. "Maybe you can answer me this, then," she said. "You said your Navy. . ."

"Coast Guard."

"Or Coast Guard picked you up at sea. They had you, had rescued you from all this. Yet they set you back down and let you fend for yourself. What do you think that was all about?"

Chancy stared across the room. The cup tilted in his hand and some of the tea spilled to the floor, but he seemed not to notice.

"I suspect that the United States can get better leverage the more of its citizens are in the middle of this mess, either loose or as hostages," I said.

"Or sympathy if some of you become casualties," Monique added.

"By tam," Rolf said. He struggled to push himself into a sitting position. Monique went to him to help.

"Well, Chancy?" I asked.

He said nothing.

"Everyone knows what world police cowboys Americans are," Jocelyn said. "You like to solve the world's problems, as long as the solution favors your way of life. You might even call it moral imperialism. You not only decide how the other countries should think about issues like drugs or weapons, but you want a say on child labor, civil rights, and ethnic cleansing. But you kindly forget that barely a hundred years ago you nearly eradicated a race because it occupied land you now occupy, and your tangle with civil rights is fresher and not perfect yet. Can you wonder that other countries find your opinions and willingness to enforce them a bit over the top?"

Chancy's head snapped up. "None of that cuts much with the way the Jamaicans are acting now that they're here."

"Have you been to Jamaica?" Jocelyn said. "Seen how people are living there. It's squalor, dirt. No wonder some of them have turned a bit violent."

Rolf said, "A bit? They're a tam sight past that, by geez-tam firecracker." He slid to the edge of the table, tried to slip off and stand, with Monique hindering him as much as helping him.

"Careful how you step when you get off there, Rolf," Chancy said. "While you were under they had you fitted with cloven hooves."

"Goot. Clop Clop." He grinned. The clean white bandage around his hand looked far better than my handiwork, though it made his hand look like a white flipper.

Chancy took out what may have been his last cigar. He bit the end, spat it into a wastebasket, reached for his lighter.

"If you plan to light that personal deflector shield," Dr. Jocelyn said, "take it outside."

Chancy glanced at Rolf and me, like we were in on

something. He went out the door of the room without looking back.

"Quiet a fella that pal of yours." Monique shook her head at me. Jocelyn was nodding about something to herself.

"He is my friend," I said. I looked at each of them, Rolf included. "And it's still my country. I may not agree with everything it, or what everyone in it does. But I live there."

In the far distance, and muffled by the walls and the air conditioning, there was an explosion.

Monique made a startled move to clutch Rolf, but stopped herself.

Jocelyn said, "I think we need to talk with Mr. Randall."

"If that involves breakfast," Rolf said, "is okay with Rolf."

The door opened and Chancy came back into the room. Tight lines formed rows across his forehead. Chancy did not have his cigar. Behind him came Malone and a man a head shorter. Malone I had seen. The other fellow, who Malone deferred to, was a compact muscular one, his head bald and shiny except for a black fringe of hair. But he looked efficient, ready. It had to be Randall. He wore khaki shorts, like the doctor, and a safari shirt with the sleeves chopped off to show his arms. He had worked on them enough. They were wiry bands-of-steel arms, the forearms covered by fine black fur. His biceps stood out like billiard balls beneath the taut flesh. I had always interpreted biceps on a man as revealing one who grabbed and pulled things toward him. Pronounced triceps, on the other hand, seemed to show me someone who pushed things away.

"Things are getting dicey, Jocelyn," he said. His eyes

swept across the rest of us, stopped when they got to Rolf's hand.

Rolf ignored the appraisal. He had gotten his feet onto the floor and took a tentative step, looked pleased to find he could still get around. He met Monique halfway to the hotplate and took the cup of bullion she offered.

"We been following it on the radio," Randall said. "From what we can make out, Johnny Be Bad's posse was run all the way up to north island where they holed up, with some of their cigarette boats ready to haul ass out of there."

Rolf put his empty cup down. He and Monique began to walk with arms over each others' shoulders in a small circle around the room like some macabre dance duo while Randall spoke. I had to tip my hat at Rolf's grit. He never complained and coped better than any of us. Monique seemed to understand and encourage the self-discipline of his rehab efforts. Whatever was to come, he was doing something about getting ready.

"It was a hostage stand-off situation all night. All hell just broke loose up there. No one can say what's coming down."

"My wife, Myrna's with one of the groups," Chancy said.

"What's worrying me," Randall said, giving Chancy a casual but eye-narrowing glance, "is where the hell Red Dreadman is. No one seems to know his whereabouts."

"I do," I said.

All heads swung to me.

"Last night," I said, "if it was that recent, we were floundering around through the woods before Haitian John found us. We passed a concealed cove where we saw boats, cigarette boats some of them, at anchor. I didn't think about it then, but every other boat we've seen on

Elbow Cay has been sunk."

"How far away was that?" Randall asked.

I told him as best I could.

"Damn." He looked at Jocelyn. "That explains the U.S. cutter standing off the shore in the sound. They've got Red bottled with his hostages. They've cut him off from making a run. Red's going to get desperate, he hears that Johnny falls."

"None of us can know how that's come out yet," Jocelyn said.

I didn't need a blueprint for the cutter's presence to lend substance to her earlier comments.

"You think they'll come here?" she asked Randall.

He shrugged. "It could cross Red's mind."

"How would they know about you way out here?" Chancy said. "We barely got here with John leading us."

"I imagine Randall may've done some business with Mr. Dreadman before," I said.

"Where do you get that?" Chancy was looking at me, head tilted a degree right.

"You ever provide any boas for him to use as mules?" I asked Randall.

"Mules?" Rolf said, his head snapping up.

"Oh, drug mules," Chancy said. Rolf straightened and leaned on Monique.

Once Chancy caught a glimmer that we were talking about something where he knew a thing or two, he was willing to lead the discussion.

"Back in '93, or so," Chancy said, "Customs at Miami found about forty pounds of coke in condoms sewn into boa rectums. That was a million street value then."

"Geez tam, butt-ache."

"They'll know you have weapons here, and a secure base," Chancy said. "Why do you have so many weapons?" he asked Randall.

"Maybe they stay clear," Rolf said, "they know you got a lot of guns."

"More likely they may want to hole up here," Jocelyn said. "They might think they would be safer here."

"You never explained all the weapons," Chancy said to Randall. His head swung to Jocelyn. "Am I missing something here?"

She raised an eyebrow, but didn't answer.

I told Chancy, "If you'd have looked in some of those cages and crates in the warehouse you just passed through, you might have seen some pretty rare creatures. In addition to the golden corn and rat Everglades snakes, I saw Oenpelli Pythons from Australia that can change colors. I saw a plowshare tortoise from Madagascar."

"And. . ." Rolf said. "So he imports, exports critters."

"Illegal ones," Chancy said, that light going off for him again. "You can get twenty, maybe thirty thousand each for any one of those."

Jocelyn was looking at me. Monique's eyes opened wider. Randall and Malone moved over to stand in front of the door, Malone's hand slipping into his pocket where I had noticed the metallic bulge.

"You know," Jocelyn said, "you two may not be helping yourselves here."

DETROIT - U.S. Fish and Wildlife Services officers, responding to an anonymous tip, made a call late yesterday evening to a Grosse Pointe residence where they confiscated a Wooley Spider Monkey said to be one of only four hundred in existence. The Wooley Spider Monkey is the largest of the New World prehensile monkeys and is native to the high forests of southeastern Brazil. The black market value of such monkeys ranges to $50,000. The USFWS continues its search for the source supplying exotic pets on the endangered list.

Chapter Ten

Randall and Malone led the way outside. The sun was brighter than I had imagined. The sky was a cloud-mottled blue. We blinked up at it and at each other. Among Rolf, Chancy and I, none of us was going to set any fashion trend.

"Hey," Chancy yelled at Sidney, "You enjoying that?"

Sidney stood from his chair. He was puffing on a cigar. "It was abandoned," he said. "I found it on the edge of the step and adopted it. It's mine now." He caught a sideways glance from Randall. "But, hey, if you wanna chew. . ." He held out the now-wet-and-gnawed end of the cigar toward Chancy.

"Forget it," Chancy said.

Randall had stopped and was watching the play. He turned and started toward the house. Monique and Dr. Jocelyn pulled up the rear. Neither of them looked as worried as I felt. Chancy looked thoughtful. Rolf was looking around in an entertained and nearly gleeful way. He was of hardy rebounding stock, I had to say.

We passed through a thick stand of banana trees and bamboo into a grove of papayas, star fruit, citrus trees. The main house had a pagoda-sloping roof leading up to a second floor with a tower and look-out deck high at the top. The wood was nature-stained cedar, a dark silvery wood that had taken the beating of weather well.

We went in a side gate to an open patio. A native in a white jacket was setting up breakfast things. There were cloths on the tables, flowers in vases on each. The flagstone patio was swept clean. On the long table that ran along the side of the patio were platters of fruit piled high, fresh biscuits, and steaming covered dishes. Rolf rushed toward them.

No matter which direction I looked, around us in the distance, or up on the tower, I could see a man carrying some kind of a gun. The place was a peaceful eye in the storm of fighting because it was the only fortified place around.

"You can clean up first, if you like," Randall said. He waved toward the half dozen small cabins on the other side of the pool. "Each has its own guest bathroom."

Chancy and I started around the pool. Rolf shoved a half dozen pieces of bacon between a biscuit he tore in half. He carried that and a bunch of grapes in his good hand as he hurried after us. "Holy tam rocking chair," he was puffing. "Food!"

We split up at the cabins, each picking one for himself. The inside of mine was small, a bed, a dresser, an open door to the bathroom. Extra towels had been placed on the end of the bed. I stripped and got into the shower. I wanted to stay in there forever. I usually think well in a shower, something about the motor cortex being busy with the mechanics of some everyday ordinary exercise that frees the mind. But after all we had been through, all I could fix on was to wonder about Randall's bringing us to the house, upgrading us to guest quarters after letting us sleep around on the floor all night.

Chancy and Rolf had both beat me back to the tables. My skin felt wrinkled and soft after all the time in the shower. I felt rejuvenated and alive from being clean after so long. It had seemed a shame to put back on the salt crusty clothes I'd been wearing.

Rolf had a plate piled high that told me I had better hurry if I was to eat at all. I went over to the long table, found conch salad and chilled crawfish tails as well as scrambled eggs, french toast. I took some of everything, and passed Rolf coming back to the table with an empty plate as I went over to sit with Chancy and Jocelyn. Paper lanterns, unlit at this sun-washed time of day, swung on their cords around us through the trees in the breeze that tugged at the ends of the tablecloths. The gentle clank of silver and tinkle of crystal contrasted with the distant steady sound of gunfire, an occasional explosion. The trees around us rustled in an unsettled way in the breeze. I could still see the armed men moving along the perimeter around us, which added to the quiet hush we felt. There was little conversation at the tables during the eating.

I was one of the first to put down my silver and sip at the coffee in its bone china cup. Randall and Monique at the other table, and then Jocelyn at my table, all gave it up. Chancy picked at bits of bacon and a biscuit. Rolf was still going as if he had just started. His eating seemed to please the native who fussed around at the food table. He brought over an entire pie to show Rolf. Rolf waved for him to put it on the table beside his plate. The native's white teeth beamed in a grin as he went back to the table.

Randall got up and went inside. When he came back out he pulled his chair over to our table, close to Chancy. "There's a lot of gunplay over there," he said. "From what we can get over the radio, there's also some negotiating going on. There was an exchange of hostage names. Your wife's name wasn't on the list."

I liked the way Randall didn't beat around about it.

Chancy nodded slowly, looking down at his empty plate. "You think she's with Red's bunch, as one of the hostages there?" he asked Randall.

Randall shrugged, realized Chancy wasn't looking at him, said, "No way of knowing."

"What are you doing about all this? Chancy asked him.

"Waiting it out."

"It's nothing to you, eh? Like one of the hurricanes that come busting through here. You tighten down the shutters and stay inside for a few days. That it?"

"Exactly." I didn't like the version of a grin that spread across Randall's face this time. "Or your stock market when it dips," he said. "The smart money that's in it for the long-term rides it out, weathers the little rough spots."

A distant explosion punctuated his sentence. I looked up at a pink and gray cloud that was getting blacker even as I looked.

"You know," Chancy said, "Pericles once said that it was not only the duty of every man to get involved in the public affairs around him, but that anyone who didn't wasn't a man."

"You can tell Pericles for me that he's an ass." Randall lowered the chair that he had tilted back onto its two back legs. He leaned closer to the table, and said in a lowered voice to Chancy, "You want to question my manhood, that's another thing."

I looked toward Chancy, afraid of what I'd see there. Some locals had put a sign out on their dock along one of the mangrove-infested canals near Hope Town that read, "No skating. Thin ice." It was a joke. But that's where I feared Chancy might take us.

The muscles along Chancy's neck knotted, then relaxed. I sighed and took a breath.

"Look," Chancy said. His eyes lifted and he leaned closer to Randall. Their eyes locked. "In the first place, we can give our promises to forget all about your place, whatever it is you do up here. In the second, if we go out there again, and do something foolhardy and get ourselves killed, that simplifies your problem even more."

"No," Jocelyn said. "That's not an option." She glared

at Chancy, then turned to look at Randall. There was tension between these two like a barbed-wire fence of electricity. It seemed to give Randall a chuckle, though she was more serious about it and glared at him with an intensity that made me want to take a step back, however immune he was to it.

"I may not have the problem you think I have," Randall said, staring back at Chancy. He leaned back in his chair and looked casual. He was not the sort of person who did "casual" well. Something behind his crocodile eyes had been doing permutations since being introduced to us.

Chancy said, "Not if you kill all of us, the women too. God knows there's been enough violence on the island already. A little more would hardly be noticed." He broke the locked stare and looked at Jocelyn, then Monique. They had turned to watch Randall.

"What do you think you could do out there?" Randall asked. His mind seemed already settled on something. I was curious to see how it would affect us.

"Try to free Myrna. If I can find her, and get to her in time."

Randall looked away in the direction of distant gunfire, or thunder. He went through the motions of thinking, but his eyes had not changed when he turned back. He looked Chancy up and down, and said, "You fancy a go at Red, do you?"

"I can't see that I have a whole lot of choice." Chancy's voice softened and his mouth turned down at the corners while he stared down at a blank spot on the tablecloth. I had never seen Chancy try to be humble before. He was not much good at it.

It seemed to amuse Randall. He turned to Jocelyn. "How's the other one, Jocelyn?"

"He's not fit to travel. These two either for that matter," she said.

"We would need our weapons back," Chancy said, getting for the first time a glimmer that Randall might really consider letting him go back out there.

"No," Jocelyn shouted. "I won't have it." She stood up, glaring at Randall.

"You won't have it?" Chancy said. He had to tilt his head at an angle to look up at her.

Randall said, "She can't decide if she's a feminist or pacifist."

"It's possible to be both," Jocelyn said from between clenched teeth.

"Not and win at anything," Randall said.

"You won't have it?" Chancy repeated.

Her angry face swung to him, and I saw more disdain that I thought anyone could be capable of showing. "You're not storming out there in the kind of adventuristic spirit that took the lot of you out shark hunting and got that man hurt." Her head snapped to Rolf. But Rolf's head was lowered and he was eating. He looked up long enough to grin, then went back to the work at hand.

"Look," Chancy said to her, "I don't know that you have much of a bloody leg to stand on, considering what you do. You don't think it strikes an odd note at all, you being a vet, claiming to have devoted your life to animals, and then your helping a man smuggle endangered animals to the highest bidder?"

"You can't begin to know what you're talking about." If Chancy was a door mat, I doubt she would have scraped her feet on him. At least that was the look she was sending his way.

Randall's head was moving as if he was at a tennis match. A smile was growing, first as a twitch at the corner of his mouth, then into a wider grin.

"If it was me," Randall said, his voice light and amused, "I'd wait until everything blows over and the scores are settled, and then check on your wife."

"But it isn't you."

"Right, so..."

"You'll let us go out there, see what we can do?"

Randall glanced around at each of us, measured Jocelyn's frown.

"Maybe I can save her," Chancy said. "Maybe it's all for nothing. But I have to know. I can't wait."

Randall was staring at Jocelyn, amused at her expression. He gave a tilt of his head and rose. The two of them, Randall and the doctor, walked away from us, stood far enough away we couldn't hear. But you didn't have to hear to read her expressions and arm waving. Randall had his back to us, but I could imagine the half smile still in place.

After a few moments Randall spun and started back, Jocelyn still in mid-sentence from the look of her. She followed him and reached out to grab at his shoulder, but he shrugged off the hand. The two of them came back and stood beside the table. Randall looked at Chancy, but Jocelyn still directed her unflinching stare at Randall.

"It's not my skin," Randall said. "You want back out there, fine with me."

Jocelyn was incredulous. Her mouth hung open for a second. Randall glared at her. There was sure something between them.

"But no weapons," Jocelyn said.

"We'll see," Chancy said.

"And I'm going with you." Jocelyn gave Chancy an unflinching glare.

"No you're not," Chancy told her.

"I will if you're to have any chance," she said. "Because I know the only way in that doesn't go through the front door." She stood up. "And," she said, "because I have to go now."

Chancy frowned. Then he thought of something, said to Randall, "Tell her no. You can't let her go out there with us. You aren't going to let her, are you?"

Randall stared at Jocelyn. He was not smiling. She stared back. He turned to look down at Chancy. "That's the deal, bucko. She goes along too, or you don't go."

* * *

It was three in the afternoon before we were all talked out and ready to go. The five of us were escorted to the gate, where Malone and Sidney handed us back the weapons and clips. I would have been as comfortable leaving my gun behind. But as it was, I took it and gave a sheepish smile back to the looks we were getting from Monique and Jocelyn. We had enough water for all of us. Jocelyn wore a small black canvas backpack, which I had figured for medical supplies. I wasn't too comfortable with their coming along. But Randall never budged from his position, and in the end we had no leverage with which to argue.

We started off through the dense growth along the narrow path. Soon, very soon, we were out of sight of the hidden Randall estate.

"He tink we all die out here, eh?" Rolf boomed. I couldn't tell if he was posturing for Monique, or if he just felt exuberant to be back closer to a hundred percent after all he'd been through. It was easy to forgive him his loud excitement.

For all their shared animosity, I had Chancy and

Jocelyn figured as an item by now. When any two people fight as much as they had, with as little provocation, it had all the earmarks to me of a budding romance.

Chancy pushed to the front of us, occasionally slashing at the leaves to the side of the path with his machete in an unnecessary way. Rolf grinned back at me, waved his white flipper. Behind me, once we had fallen far enough to the rear of the others, Jocelyn said, "Is your friend Chancy always like this?"

"He does seem a touch closer to his dark side right now," I whispered, "but give it time. He's got good in him."

Monique gave me a smile that carried a little tension as she slipped around me on the path and went up to join Rolf.

"Hope it doesn't get us killed," Jocelyn said.

"Something to wish for," I agreed. Walking this close to her, I caught the full impact of her eyes. Something in them drew me to a prominent white scar I saw that ran down from under her t-shirt sleeve all the way to her elbow and under her forearm. The dots of the stitches showed. Her eyes made me want to ask how she had hurt herself. I realized that there was something, some shadow behind the strength of her eyes that was as close to the memory of pain as I had ever seen.

We hiked steadily, through more mosquitoes and gnats than I recalled ever seeing in the Bahamas before. It was another hour and a half before we paused and took a break.

I watched the others past my tilted water bottle. All of us, even Chancy, seemed to be having second thoughts. We looked as far removed from anything like a strike force as you could ask for. Each of us had lowered to the dirt of the wide spot in the path. Rolf sprawled, happy as if at a picnic.

Our pace had been slow enough for me to note the moist green of each leaf, the sting of an occasional leaf's edge sweeping across one of my sweat-covered forearms, or a gnarl of root sticking up in the pressed-dirt footpath that had been formed by barefoot natives rather than people like us. There had been time enough to think, but not to understand.

Sitting on the dirt, huddled with the others along the trail, I watched beads of sweat form on my arms as soon as I wiped them, and I struggled to make more sense of what was going on, what we hoped to accomplish.

We had made a big leap somewhere and I wasn't sure that if I'd been rested and not still half in shock if I could have paid more attention and understood what was going on. I could understand where Chancy was going and why, but not why the two women were suddenly along. My head throbbed, and the gentle rustling of leaves in the tops of the coconut trees was like the confusing hum of insects to me.

We could hear only an occasional shot or two in the far distance. The showdown with Johnny Be Bad was still in progress. We had no way of knowing how the negotiations were going there. I had to agree with Randall, who had felt that all of the Bahamian forces were focused on one of the groups at a time.

The gun I held was sweaty and warm to my touch by now, but I was glad to have it along after all. I looked at Monique. She was a bit pale beneath her tan, sweating and looking good while doing it. Dr. Jocelyn sat staring at the trail ahead, brooding. I think all of us, except Chancy, could have been swung to mutiny if it had not been for Rolf.

After the meal, Rolf had gotten back some of himself,

more than before perhaps. He chuckled, kidded the women, even gave Chancy a goat barb now and then. It made me admire and like him more than ever. Here he was, the hurt one of us, the one who had the least reason to be along on this phase of the silliness so far, and he was making a party of it while we sulked around with the half empty glass.

To tell the bone truth, I don't know how Rolf did it, unless it was having been divorced three times before and having lost everything. I know I dwelled on the very recent sense of having lost my marriage, and on having lost passport, money, everything I had brought on the trip as well. On top of that, to be facing a situation where I could lose more, much more. I had only to look at Jocelyn and Monique to sense that they were taking some inventories of their worldly status too. We all were in a funk. All except Rolf. He sat now looking around us with a smile until his glance landed on Chancy. "You mind I ask you one ting?" he said.

"What?" Chancy lifted his lowered head.

"When we were back at the house. You said wifey was gone."

"Yeah?"

"I look around too, you know. I don't see any of her tings. What you tink . . .?"

Chancy was struggling to his feet.

"Hey," I said, shouted really. "Let's hear him out. Is what he's saying true, Chance?"

He didn't answer at first. He looked up the trail, then panned the faces of each of us. He seemed to be sweating more than any of us. "No," he said at last. He stared directly at me. "I didn't see any of her things. Nothing of hers was destroyed."

"Oh, this just gets better and better," Jocelyn yelled.

She stood upright faster than I could have managed. "You don't even know that she was taken hostage."

"Why're you hauling all of us along on what could be a goose chase?" Monique said.

Chancy looked cornered. He was off center, which was unlike him as I had ever seen before in all my years of knowing him. His head bowed. I thought for a second he was going to cry. Oh, please, oh please, I thought, don't let him cry.

He looked up, his shoulders squared. "You can all go along," he said, "or you can stay. But I'm going there, see what I can do. Even if she's not there. I'll go it alone if I have to."

Jocelyn just shook her head.

Monique glanced at Jocelyn, and said, "I guess we ain't got much of a choice." She gave a glance back at Randall's estate, then started to gather up her things.

"No, I guess we haven't," Jocelyn said. She spun and started walking.

I stood and slipped my small pack back over my shoulder. Rolf had already turned and started up the trail toward where Dreadman was holed up.

Chancy stepped up his pace until he was walking beside Jocelyn. We all grouped into a tighter ball as we moved ahead toward a bigger mess than we had left behind.

"Look," he said, "I didn't ask you two to come along. The both of you should have stayed back there." Jocelyn kept walking. "Maybe she's held captive, and maybe she isn't. But it's up to me to find out, not you. Go back if you like. You know that I'd prefer that you both did. You heard me back there. But it was you insisted on coming."

"What is it with you?" Jocelyn said without looking at him. She stood tall, almost but not quite up to Chancy's face, if she cared to look his way. Her eyes flashed, though her hands swung at her sides. A thin sheen of sweat made her face glisten. She looked like some dark-haired Norse goddess. How Chancy could just walk beside her and not notice her more was beyond me. He looked straight ahead.

"Either way," he said, and paused, "I have to know."

Jocelyn let out a half snort of air and picked up her stride until she was walking ahead and didn't have to see him.

"*I'm not just trying to get through life, or to conquer it. But I would like to savor it, like that first taste of butterscotch on the tongue, a whiff of pine high in some woods, or the calming sound of water running down across rocks in some fern-lined stream. What about you, Monique?"*

"What you need is variety, or sometimes doing without so that getting feels good again."

"Like hitting yourself on the head with a hammer because it feels so good when you quit?"

"That's one version."

Chapter Eleven

We came in from a higher elevation than before. Elbow Cay is not a mountainous island. But it has its bare bone coral and limestone hills, each covered with dense jungle growth – cacti, razor-edged young coconut trees, gnarly scrub bushes that can take the salt and anything a person could throw their way. We took another rest where two paths crossed.

Below us, the cove held its half dozen bobbing boats – a couple of cigarette boats and other deep sea fast craft gathered up by Dreadman's posse during all the earlier raiding. The mansion was a sandy-colored stone block building, modelled after a castle. It sat to the right of the cove. A matching stone bridge arched over to a small island where a three-story lookout tower stood. It was built of the same stone and had Tudor arches, ramparts, and a parapet walk. They had mounted a machine gun on a tripod in the lookout. I could see the multi-colors of a hat and shirt of someone resting in the shadows near the gun.

Out in the sound, a good five hundred feet from the cove's hidden mouth, beyond the deeper-water buoy, sat the U.S. cutter, at anchor. I could see small figures moving about, but in the motion of routine cleaning chores. It was just there.

Monique went over to my left and sat on a coconut tree's trunk that was bent at a right angle sideways before starting upward. Its bole made a good seat. She plopped down on it. Chancy was down the trail to my right, looking down at the enclosed fortress of the mansion's courtyard and inner grounds. He and Jocelyn had their heads together and were talking. She had been to the mansion before to care for pets. Rolf squatted on the dirt of the trail and pulled a biscuit sandwich from his bag. He worked on that.

I went to Monique and sat down on the tree trunk beside her, let the breeze sweep over us for a few minutes while we both watched small whitecaps ripple across the blue and white water of the sound. Coconut trees swayed around us and rustled in the wind.

"Do you ever wonder," I asked, "if other people feel the same way as you about their being in your life?"

"You suffering from some 'Center of the Universe' syndrome?" she said without turning her head to me.

It hit me like a slap. I couldn't figure out what I'd done to make both women so sulky and surly around me. They weren't giving Rolf a hard time, and stayed away from Chancy as much as they could.

"No. I don't think so," I said. I heard, then watched a hummingbird buzz to a tree near us and hover in front of an orange trumpet vine bloom. "I admit to being a late bloomer, getting to the big picture at a somewhat older age than other people I know. But I'm pretty well over the notion that the world was designed for me, and other people orbit around my life."

"That's good."

"It's just that sometimes I don't always get everyone else's motivation, what makes them do what they do, what drives them on. I mean Jocelyn, for instance. What motivates her? She never shares that."

"Oh, and you do?" She stared off into the swaying tips of trees.

"I do."

"Well, not on purpose."

"It's just that I can understand Chancy, Rolf, and me coming out here, whether it's a ridiculous quest or not. But I don't understand a doctor coming with us."

"And a waitress," Monique said, "or doesn't that cut

anything?"

"Okay. And a waitress too – a future doctor for all I know."

Even that didn't make her turn. "You know," she said, "you're not the original you think you are. You watch people all day long as much as I have, and listen, you'd figure that out. Hell, if you think us being out here is your plan, or Chancy's, you're wrong. You don't know him like I do."

"Who, Randall?"

"Who else?"

Her head turned slowly to look at me. Her eyes were very brown. An attractive light sheen of sweat still clung to her smooth tanned cheeks, a trickle of sweat running down to her chin. I was aware that I was in the same clothes I had worn for a long time.

"You want to know what's attractive about your friend Chancy?" she said. "I mean apart from his having eyes like light blue topaz gems."

I don't recall if I nodded or just sat there and stared back at her.

"It's his desire," she said. "No matter if he's dead ass right or wrong, or what, there is a man with a fire in his belly. He probably knows he's being manipulated, but getting out of there was the only way to fight against it."

"And that's attractive?"

"Damn straight."

"That's why you're along?"

"No," she said. She turned back to look at the sound. In the far distance we could see the dark line of Abaco Island, the city of Marsh Harbour, the airport. "I'm with Dr. Jocelyn. That and not wanting to stay back there with Mr. Randall."

"You don't trust him?"

She didn't look at me, or answer.

I repeated the question. She looked up, then over at me. Leaning closer, for an intimate whisper, she said, "He let us come out here with you bent dicks, didn't he?"

She hopped off the coconut trunk and walked toward the others, her hips swaying with just a touch of irritated snap to each swing.

I eased off the trunk and went over to Rolf. He was leaning back on his elbows letting the sun beam down on his already red face.

"What's the matter with her?" I dropped down into a squat beside him.

He blinked the slits of his eyes, turned to look at me. "Don't vant to die maybe."

I stood up and started down the trail.

"Where you going?" he asked.

"To look for a goat for you."

I stopped when I was beside Chancy and Dr. Jocelyn. He turned to me, said, "She knows a way in, a cut through the lava from the boat area. But it's guarded. She thinks we ought to wait until it's darker, and I agree." He called over to Rolf, "That okay with you?"

"Fine. I tink Rolf takes a nap." He lay back where he was on the path.

"Watch for ants, Rolf," Jocelyn said.

"We're right on two crossing paths," Chancy said to me. He was looking into me, maybe seeing if what was left of me was up to this. I don't know. "One of us should watch from each end, let the others know if there's any foot traffic coming our way."

"Okay." I said. "I'll take the side closest to the fortress, or whatever it is." I looked around. The vegetation got thicker just off the trail on either side. I don't know where we were going to run if we did get someone coming at us.

Jocelyn was looking at me closely too, weighing me it seemed. Part of me wanted to tell her that I had already killed men. The other part wanted no part of thinking or talking about that. These were strong-willed women, more so than anything I'd come across in the cutthroat business world back in the city. And I was coming to feel that I knew as little about them as I did my way around through the jungle that surrounded us.

I started down the trail that narrowed to a green tube of plant life. I turned a sharp right and a left and came to another small opening that looked out over the cove. Monique stood there. She stared out at nothing, her arms crossed. I slowed and went closer. I wanted to reach out a hand to her, but didn't dare. I stood close beside her and looked down at the stone building. I said nothing.

After a few minutes she seemed to notice me for the first time, gave me that "you again" look.

She said, "Rolf mentioned that your wife left you, that it happened during this trip."

"Yeah, this vacation's been a real benchmark as bummers go so far."

"What did you like about being married?"

"What?"

"I mean, was it having someone to come home to, or what?"

"I don't know what you're getting at."

"Well, was there an exchange of needs, the working together, the talking, the sharing, supporting and understanding each other?"

"I'm not sure why we're suddenly talking about that."

"With you halfway hitting on me, I just wondered what went wrong with the relationship you had."

"Why don't we just cut through some of this," I was

starting to feel a little testy myself, "and you tell me what you think's wrong with me."

"Well," she dragged out, "you judge."

"Me?'

"All the time. You wanna evaluate all the time, know where every other fella stands. No one ever told you before?"

"My ex-wife."

"Why'd she leave you?"

"I don't really know."

"You see, that's it. That's all of it."

"I don't get it."

"And you never will."

"Try me."

She looked away, then back at me. "You not only judge, but you judge too quickly. You trust your instincts, and in your case you shouldn't, 'cause you're not as aware of what's going on around you as you think."

"Is that all?" I tried to make it chipper, but it was hard when my insides felt like a churning wheel of guts full of broken glass.

If she could sense how I felt she didn't show it. She said, "You're a person who needs help but isn't good about asking for it, or graceful about receiving it."

We could have gone on like that, but I would have just as soon mashed my fingers in a door. I hung my head a bit, said, "I guess I'm pretty much damaged goods, eh?"

"You said it, not me," she said.

I looked up, my mouth opening, then closing.

"Answer me this," she said. "You say Chancy is your friend. What is there about him you like?"

I started to speak and stopped. I turned my head, looked out to the water, the building, the trees. I turned back. "He just is."

"You accept a lot about him, accommodate that?"

"I don't know what you're getting at."

"Look," she said. She stepped closer, reached to turn my head until I stared right at her, deep into her wet brown eyes. She kept her warm hands on the sides of my face. "Back there, when Randall suddenly takes us to the house, treats you like guests after letting you spend the night on the floor. Did you understand any of that?"

"No," I admitted.

"But you went along. The others seemed to understand, so you went, never said a damn thing."

I didn't say anything. So she went on, " Did you figure one of them understood?" She nodded up the trail. "It certainly wasn't sweet ol' Rolf. It was a meal to him."

"Where are you going with this?" I managed.

"So here we are, in the middle of some macho bullshit, getting ready to face down Red Dreadman and his posse, some truly bad people who kill as casually as you'd squash a scorpion under a boot, and you're just going along with the flow, don't really know why, just one of the guys."

"I know why. It's for Chancy's wife."

"Who may not even be down there."

"If all this bothers you so much," I said, "why don't you just leave. You and Jocelyn take off and hide somewhere until it's all over."

"I can't. We can't."

"Why?"

"Because we have thought about it. We're in it, like it or not."

"You haven't made any of this more clear to me," I said.

She let go of the sides of my face and pushed around me. "Well, you have a lot of time to think about it."

"You didn't have to come with us, you know, Jocelyn."

"Let's not talk about what I did or didn't have to do anymore."

"Suits me."

"You really like this life and death stuff, don't you, Chancy."

"The life part."

Chapter Twelve

For what seemed a year or two I stood in the path listening to every sound the growth around me had to share. Things rustled, popped, made small crashes. In the distance I could still hear a shot or two fired.

A rustle behind me up the trail snapped me around. It was Rolf. He carried a large green coconut and the machete Chancy had been flailing earlier. He grinned at me as mischievously as some goat-footed Pan from mythology. He held the coconut out to me, shook it. I could hear liquid sloshing around inside. "Ripe one," he said.

He looked down at the enclosure below, out at the boats, the small ones in the cove, the cutter farther out. "What you tink?" He plopped to the path and pulled over an inch-thick fallen limb. He held the stick between his feet, began cutting it into a stump of a stake, sharpening each end into a point.

I looked out to the water. The sky had been an unblemished blue a moment before. Now, small black clouds had appeared, slanting lines of rain coming down from each of them as they drifted across the sound. The clouds bunched, became a bigger black blob coming our way.

"I've been up here trying to decide if we're all incredibly naive, or if we just have some over-developed sense of justice."

Rolf shoved one pointed end of the stake into the ground so that its spike stood up. He held the coconut with his flipper and good hand and brought it down toward the stake. But he didn't strike it. He held the coconut to me.

I could imagine what a shock a blow like that would have been to his injured hand. I put my gun down and hoisted the coconut, brought it down hard on the stake. A whole side of the green husk ripped loose and fell away, revealing the brown hard shell inside. I turned the coconut in my hands. Each time I brought it down more of the husk loosened or fell away. When only the brown center was left, he motioned for me to lay it on the path. He brought the back of the machete blade down on it hard. It cracked. I didn't think about the noise he was making until then. I looked around. Nothing.

I reached for it, lifted it, saw the cracks running in three directions. I twisted the nut hard in my hands. It wrenched open. I pulled the two halves apart, was able to save most of the milk. I poured it into the two halves until they were equal. I held one out to him. We both drank.

He took the end of the machete, holding the half between his feet, and began to try and work loose some of the meat from his half. "Here," I said. I took it from him, pried with the blade. A large chunk popped loose. He grabbed it and began to chew off chunks. I cut a piece out of the other half and chewed it. The meat was very rich, like hardened chunks of the white fat you see on the edge of a top sirloin. It tasted full of fat and calories, which was fine with us.

"What do you think?" I said between chews.

"Goot," he said.

"I mean about what we're up to?"

He didn't answer, but chewed and looked thoughtful.

"There's a lot about being in a tropical paradise you don't always get to think about," I said.

A small dark scorpion started across the path toward us. Whether it was after some of the coconut or us I couldn't say. Rolf reached for the machete and smashed the flat of the blade down on it.

"There's the heat rash," I said, "and bugs, thorns, cactus needles, poisonwood, the sun . . . and scorpions." I looked down at the wet spot in the path. "And here we are, two and a half men and a couple of women on the edge of PMS thinking we can take on a gang of drug-running killers."

"I hope the half means you," he said. He grinned as he chewed.

"Sure," I said, a little too quickly.

"And is not PMS, with Monique" he said. "Is yust no tam tating game either."

"Dating game? She thinks that?" I said.

Rolf shoved an even bigger piece of coconut into his mouth.

"So I stand up here," I said, "wondering if I could shoot anyone again, if I had too. I don't know, and I don't think so. The first time it was more of an accident. At least that's the way it plays back in my memory."

"Tam accurate accident," Rolf laughed. "Maybe you half more lucky accidents later." He found that even funnier.

When I didn't respond, he said, "You tink too much. By geez-tam, we all be busy soon enough."

"That's just it," I came close to shouting at him. "One says I should think more, the other less. Just what. . .?"

"You choose," Rolf said. He picked up the machete and his half of the coconut and began to struggle to his feet. "None of my tam concern."

He walked back up the trail, left me to my thoughts, hopes, expectations, such as they were. I had barely turned to look back down at the fortress when I heard scurrying behind me. I spun. It was Rolf. He waved the machete and pointed behind him with his white flipper. He came panting to me, bent to take a breath or two. He straightened, his face flushed red. "Gone," he said. "Gone, by geez-tam monkey bars."

He had only his machete. I had the gun I held and what spare clips were in my pack. I glanced down behind us, then nodded up the trail, took the lead and eased slowly around each curve in the trail until I was in the crossed trail opening where we had gathered before. Nothing.

Rolf and I split up, each heading left and right on the trail we had not yet followed. Thirty yards down the trail there was a spot in the loose dirt where I could make out a bare footprint. The steps led down the slope away from us.

I went back to the opening. Rolf was there, shaking his head. I nodded back the way I had come.

He looked around on ground, saw something that made him jump. He ran forward, bent and grabbed at something. He held it up. It glittered silver in the sun. I came closer and looked. It was Chancy's lighter.

Above the sound of sporadic gunfire a shriek pierced the clammy afternoon calm air before the storm.

There was a rustle in a towering strangler fig, then color burst from the green cover, outlined against the tumble of dark cloud fists in the sky.

Green wings spread and flapped as the Bahama parrot circled and lifted, its red throat and the blue underside of its wings and tail exposed as it climbed higher.

There were few enough of its kind left, and it was a toss-up if this one would return.

It shrieked again and began to flap away, out across the angry white-capped skin of the ocean toward the distant Amazon.

Chapter Thirteen

I reached for the lighter. It was hot, whether from the sun or Chancy's pocket I couldn't tell. I wondered if there had been a struggle.

It's odd. You hold an object from someone, some thing the person used every day and it's in your hand, all that you have of them there. I was still not over being seven years old and having my father's silver watch handed to me after the military funeral, the red and white stripes of the flag being folded into a triangle, guns being fired into the air. But I was thinking of Chancy in the past tense. I stopped myself.

"Geez and Mary," Rolf said.

"What?" I looked up. Monique came around the bend of the upper end of the trail. She saw us, glanced around in the opening where we stood, began to run as she came closer.

"Where. . .?" she panted.

"Rastas half them," Rolf said, cutting right to it. I was working on a nicer, more speculative way to say it.

"Come on," I waved an arm and took off on the downward path where I had seen the prints of bare feet. "Keep it quiet."

I heard Monique's loud whispering to Rolf behind me. I caught Jocelyn's name. Ahead on the trail alarmed birds took off in a whirring flap of wings, crying out in several different screeches. The prickly vegetation around us got denser the farther we went. Before I could wave back for her to be more quiet, Rolf got through to her. All I could hear was their soft hurried steps.

Anyone moving with hostages would be moving slower

than we could. I stepped faster until I was twenty yards ahead of Rolf and Monique. The hill was steep. I might not have caught a glimpse of them ahead if the trail did not meander in switchbacks down the slope. I caught a bare glimmer of multi-color through the thick brush and stopped.

I dropped low on the trail, signalled for Rolf to stay back. I crawled forward on hands and knees, edging around until I could peek ahead. I saw one lookout posted. He stood looking back up the trail. A small white cloud was near his face before the breeze whisked it away. Ganja. The others would be stopped for a rest on the trail ahead I hoped.

I slithered back until I was out of sight. Then I stood and sprinted to where Rolf and Monique stood. Rolf's eyes were in an attentive squint. Monique's brown eyes were as wide as I've ever seen them. "Did you. . . ?" she started to whisper.

I waved her still. To Rolf I said, "Can you cut some of those two-way stakes like you made to husk the coconut, only smaller, stick them in the ground by that tree we passed a hundred feet back up the hill? We'll need a lot of them."

"Enough to cover the trail?" He winked. "Sure ting."

I led the way back to the spot. Rolf and I picked up finger-thick sticks as we went. We stopped where the trail narrowed. The leaning trunk of a coconut tree bent out toward the path. If you pushed aside a frond of thick leaves you could slip around outside the tree. It was shady and dim along the trail, also good.

Rolf dropped to his knees and started on the stakes. As he finished each one of them he shoved one pointed end into the ground leaving a sharp point sticking up. He was pressing them in so that there was barely an inch of space between them. Perfect.

"If Chancy and Jocelyn come tearing up this trail," I whispered to Monique, "your job will be to wave them to the outside of the tree. Once they're around it, all of you get moving."

"But what's. . .?"

"Rolf'll explain." Hearing myself made me think of a line that went like, "Shut up, he explained." Monique was not looking at me as if I was as much a jerk as that. But that did not help the way I felt. There was no time.

I turned and hurried back down the trail. The storm clouds were moving in closer for a mid-afternoon torrent. Fine with me. Great, in fact.

I slowed at the turn in the trail, eased close enough to see the Rasta still on lookout at his post. I eased back, careful to make no sudden movement.

To the right of the trail, the growth was nearly impenetrable. All I could see were stickers, knife-edged sharp leaves, spider webs, and the moist mucky soil. Thinking about it wasn't going to make it any easier. While I still had enough light I checked the selector switch on the AK-47, moved it from safety at the top click to semi-automatic at the bottom. I'd learned the automatic setting earlier.

I pushed into the thick plant wall, was stopped only a step or two in, had to slide right and work back and forth as I pressed deeper. It was dark, damp, and hot in the thick of all that green. I was ten feet in, and moving as carefully as I could to avoid noise when the approaching storm hit. Water hammered down onto me, around me, and, it felt, through me. Rain poured over my hair and face, blinded me, soaked my clothes, beat down the near leaves and plant tops. It didn't make the going any easier, but it did cover the sound I was making.

Before, with insects crawling over me and flying into me and around me, with sweat running down my face and some in a trickle down my back, I had felt every cut of every leaf, every bruise as I slipped in the muck and banged into something hard. I had been miserable then. Busy, but miserable. Now I felt worse.

You come down to the Bahamas thinking of white sand beaches, cruising in a boat with the sun and wind sweeping across you. You forget that there is sometimes a yin to the yang. But I would be pressed to say when I've been more unhappy with the tropics than I was just then – the rain knifing into my face, the rest of me wrestling through a mat of sharp, cutting, ripping, stabbing jungle. Then my left foot slipped in the ooze below. My leg shot off at an angle that wrenched my knee. Pain shot up and down the leg. I hoped the knee was just hyper-extended. I tried to press ahead, and found I could not put weight on that leg or lift it.

I stood in the downpour, took off my belt, and wrapped it around the knee. All this in the cramped vise of dripping plants and the pour of rain. I wrapped the belt criss-cross around the knee and tied it off in a knot. Then I tried to press forward again. I couldn't. I had to unwrap the knee, make a slip knot of the belt by passing the end through the buckle. By holding the end of the belt with my left hand I could lift the leg and take a step, painful, but forward. I pushed at the wet green wall in my face with the hand holding the AK-47. I pressed on. Blade leaves cut me, stickers stabbed, but I staggered onward, lifting my bum leg. The roar of the rain made me as good as deaf. I nearly overshot my goal. A low flicker of color ahead warned me just in time. The guard on the trail had hunched down to wait out the rain.

I tried to rush forward, and felt the claws of the jungle

green locked onto me. I twisted, pushed at the limbs clinging to me. On the path, the multi-colored hat was rising. Even in the downpour the sentry must have heard my thrashing.

I lunged, pain shooting up and down my leg. The thorns holding me tore loose. I surged forward, burst through the last few feet of green knives, stumbled onto the path. Hard as the rain had been coming down in the thicket, it was worse on the path, almost impossible to see through. I could make out the blur of the Rasta guard lifting his weapon and swinging it toward me.

I snapped my gun up, squeezed the shot, and saw him lifted into the air, his gun dropping to the path. He crumpled into the thick green on the other side, hidden from view. I picked up his gun. The safety was still on. I clicked it to semi-automatic and turned to go down the path, found I had to hunch forward, holding the belt end in my teeth while I hobbled holding a gun in each hand. I was glad I didn't have to look at myself as I tottered through each painful hunch-backed step. I forced myself to go as fast as I could, knew the blast of my single shot might have carried through the downpour.

The trail was mud, and slick. I rushed around the next bend and almost into the huddled group. I saw them too late, tried to stop and slid, fell to the ground in as ungraceful a pile as a human can. The slip saved my life.

The Rasta in front of me rose, spun, and began firing, mowing the leaves behind me in a line. From where I lay, I squirmed to my side and squeezed one round from the gun in my left hand. It spun him around and dropped him. As he fell, Chancy leaped up from where he was squatted in the trail and scrambled for the weapon. Chancy's hands were tied at the wrists, but that barely slowed him.

Behind him, her mouth hanging open a bit, Jocelyn

stared at me. Another guard was behind her – the last of them from the look of it. He swept an arm to Jocelyn to push her aside and out of his way. His gun was already leveled. I expected to see the flash from its barrel at any second, as soon as the barrel cleared Jocelyn. I couldn't get a clear shot without risking hitting her, and hoped Chancy wouldn't try even if he could work his gun with bound hands.

Jocelyn surprised me, and the guard even more, by standing up and wrenching the gun from the guard's hands. She swung it at him, hit him in the throat, below the open mouth that gaped at her. His mouth snapped shut, then open, flapped as he fell backwards into the brush while trying to breathe.

"That all of them?" I called to Chancy. "I got the one up the trail from you."

"Yeah," he called. He was fumbling at the fallen man near him, stood with a knife he pulled from the man's sheath, started on the rope wrapped around his wrists. He said to Jocelyn, "I wish you'd have let me take care of that one." He was glaring at me.

Her head was frozen on the spot where her guard had sailed into the green. Her face snapped to us, all of her earlier self-possessed calm gone. "Either of you have a pencil? I might be able to do a trache, save him."

I hobbled over, pushed the leaves aside, looked down at him through the hammering rain. He lay on his back, his mouth opening and closing, his hands grabbing at his throat.

Jocelyn pushed me aside and moved down toward him. She held the knife she had snatched from Chancy. The bonds on her wrists were cut loose. I saw the man's eyes open wider. He thought, like me, that she was going to finish him off. She pushed aside the thorny limb of a bush and squatted down beside the fallen Rasta. She winced for only a second when the limb snapped into her back.

I moved closer, thought I might have to be handy if there was a struggle. Rain poured over my back, sheltering her a bit. She ignored me.

The Rasta was staring at her, trying to push back from her, but too weak. Part of his panic was from not being able to breathe. But his eyes were fixed on the knife.

Jocelyn grabbed at a small twig, whittled an end quickly to a point. She bent closer and stabbed the Jamaican in the center of his neck with it. She yanked it back out. There was a gasping sucking sound I could hear over the pounding rain. From her shirt pocket she pulled a plastic ball-point pen. She unscrewed it, pulled off the front end, and pushed the narrowed end with its small hole into the Rasta's throat. She held it there. Bubbles of blood and foam shot out, then I heard the gasping, sucking noise. The Rasta's eyes had begun to roll back in his head, showing only white. Now they cleared. He looked up at Jocelyn. His eyes were bloodshot and still open wide.

She held the tube in place until his breathing got more regular. He started to struggle and try to get to his feet, but she pressed a hand flat on his chest and held him still. She shook her head and he stopped moving.

"Here," she said to me. "Hold this."

I went down onto my good right knee. I dropped the gun I held in my right hand behind me, out of reach. He flinched, but did not have enough back yet to move as I reached and held the tube in place. She slipped off her backpack, held it so the rain would not pour in. She dug until she came out with a roll of tape.

The Rasta still struggled to breathe regularly. Jocelyn reached over and pulled out the plastic tube. His eyes snapped even wider and he struggled, bubbling gasps coming from the hole at his neck. The blood was washed away at once by the pour of the rain.

Jocelyn cut off the end of the ball point tube a bit, making the end hole larger. She slipped it back in place. I held it there while she cut off strips of tape with the knife.

She shoved the knife into the ground at her ankle, reached and began putting the strips around the tube. It was good medical tape. It held even in the downpour.

He was stirring more, getting more air, and perhaps a bit of water. She bent closer, said to him, "Can you breathe now?"

He gave a curt nod. Rain poured down across his face. His eyes stayed locked with hers.

"You do good work," I said to her.

"It's why I'm along," she said.

"It be. . ." the Jamaican's husky whisper of a voice was hard to hear over the rain. Jocelyn bent closer. The blow and repair was below his voice box. That was good. "It be one grate-ful mon's life you save," he rasped. His hand slid forward, squeezed her hanging hand softly. "I be near sittin' wit the Natty Dread dere, I was." He looked up at her in a tender and thankful way that must make a doctor feel as good as she can.

I saw just a flicker in his eyes. It made me lean closer. His hand let go of hers and grabbed at the knife handle. He tugged it out of the ground and spun her with his other hand, clenched her as a shield and lifted the knife, its point poised over her chest.

My hand was lifting. I shoved the barrel of the gun in my left hand right to his face. He dropped the knife, grabbed at the barrel. As he wrenched it forward, my finger squeezed the trigger. The barrel was at his face. The shot blew off a third of his forehead. He fell back and his other hand dropped from Jocelyn.

She wriggled loose, pulled herself to her knees and spun to look at him. "You. . . You. . . ." She was panting, her head snapping back and forth from the dead Rasta to me.

Without looking any more at me, she grabbed her medicine bag and struggled to her feet. It was harder for me to get to mine. I got both the guns and the knife, put the knife in my belt and slung one of the guns over my shoulder. I hobbled out onto the path using one gun butt as a cane, the other hand lifting the belt around my knee. Where my upper and lower leg met at the knee, it felt like rusty twisted pieces of metal grating against each other.

"What's the hell's the matter with you?" Chancy said, looking at my leg.

Jocelyn sat slumped in the path, her bag dropped loosely beside her on the path. Her head turned slowly toward me, saw me struggling. She got slowly to her feet, came over to me, dropped to her knees in front of me. She would not look up at me. Her focus was on my knee.

"You know, adversity is supposed to strengthen, not weaken the warrior," Chancy said. There was a bit of edge in his voice. He bent over Jocelyn's shoulder.

"Shut up," she said to Chancy without looking up at him. "Just shut the hell up."

"What?" he said.

Now she looked up, and if I was him, I would have rather she hadn't. "You don't want to go there," she said.

Whatever was in her eyes reminded me of an argument Dashell Hammett once had with Lillian Hellman. At one point in the argument he had lifted a cigarette and began twisting it out in one of his cheeks. "Why are you doing that?" she said. He said back to her, without stopping, "To keep from doing it to you."

Ill advised as it was, Chancy said, "I suppose you'd rather still be a hostage."

She had turned back to my knee. Her face snapped up toward his. "Yes," she said, without hesitation. "I would far rather be kidnapped and held hostage than be responsible for the death of any living thing."

"I don't believe that," Chancy said, "any more than I think you were unaware that your helping Randall is in direct conflict with your save-every-life credo."

Through clenched teeth, and with her silver eyes like bullets, Jocelyn said, "I would do whatever I have to do to help any living creature, even a human, even you. But it would take a lot before I sink to this raw macho adventuristic level that seems to motivate you, and Mr. Randall." She turned back to look at my throbbing leg.

Chancy didn't respond.

The knee was a little swollen, and hurt where she touched it. I bit my lip and kept my mouth shut, handed the spare gun over to Chancy. He took the knife back too. He gave me another glare, but said nothing.

She wrapped the knee with tape, and knew what she was doing. This time when I tried to take a step, it could hold my weight. Chancy brought over a stick he had cut as a walking staff. I gave it a quick glance to make sure he hadn't gotten poisonwood, by accident or on purpose. But it was ironwood, and as good a staff as you could ask for. We started back up the trail.

In the brief glances I got of Jocelyn's face, she looked beaten and sad. I could not tell in the downpour if there were tears, or if it was the rain running down her cheeks.

We turned the last stretch of path leading to the trap I'd had them set. Rolf and Monique were huddled in the path over a man with thin black sticks of legs and arms. We got closer. It was Haitian John.

"Now what?" Jocelyn moaned.

"He come runnin' down the path the other way," Monique said.

"Got caught in the trap we set," Rolf said.

"Who set a trap?" Jocelyn's face swung to me, to Chancy. When she looked back to John she did not step forward. Her eyelids fluttered. She dropped to her knees with a muddy thud. She stared off into the rain that surrounded us at nothing, but I don't think I have ever seen a face such a mix of tired, mad, sad before.

"Don't look at me," Chancy said. "I haven't killed or harmed a single person yet."

"Doc," Monique said, in a sharp snapping voice meant to get through to Jocelyn. "Think of your parents."

Jocelyn's face looked more hurt and disoriented as it swung to Monique. "I told you to never. . ."

"I mean," Monique's head tilted toward John.

"Oh," Jocelyn said. Her hair was matted and the rain poured over her.

"We got the ones out of the bottoms of his feet," Monique said, "but there's a couple still in his shoulder yet where he fell."

The rain began to ease at last. I could not tell if I heard Jocelyn sigh, but believed I did. She stirred, shook her head the tiniest bit and got out a swab and began to clean the wounds on John's feet. The rain eased to a mist.

Chancy and Rolf stood side by side a few steps away. Chancy nodded for me to come closer. When I hobbled over, he leaned toward me and said in a low voice, "You know, you're putting egg on my face."

I felt my face flush, even in the rain. I said, "Maybe you could hang a strip of bacon from each ear. Then everyone will think the egg's there on purpose."

Rolf began to chuckle, but stopped when Chancy

turned to stare at him.

I stared at Chancy. "I know that you want to be the cavalry, the white knight. But there's been no other way to play it so far."

Chancy's face got darker in the steady drizzle. He spun on a heel and started over to where Jocelyn was bent over John. Rolf turned and went with him.

"Is not too bright," I heard Rolf mutter, "but is one crack shot, by geez-tam."

"From point-blank range? I scarcely see how he could have missed." All this loud enough for me to hear. He said something else, in a lower tone to Rolf. I caught a scrap, ". . .lacks the instinct for this kind of thing."

I took a few deep misty breaths, moved closer. Monique took a sideways step to let me into the huddle. But she did not look at me. Jocelyn glanced up from her work at me.

"Is this the only way you could think of doing this?" she snapped suddenly at me.

"I've just been trying to do the right thing," I said. "These Jamaicans. . ."

"Well, I guess you *did* save us." There was the same disdain in the tone that she used whenever she said "Mister" Randall. "But you killed every one of them doing it."

My knee was throbbing like it had a life of it's own, and I could barely stand. But any joy I thought I might have savored over rescuing them was gone.

"There are good people in Jamaica, you know," she said. "Just as there are here, or in the states."

"We have a few bad ones too," Chancy said. He had bent closer and was watching her work.

She ignored him, which seemed to bother him more, and she stared up at me a few more seconds before going back to her work. "This is the kind of thing I thought I might prevent by coming along. I guess I was fooling myself about that." She had to hold herself back from wrapping John's wound's too tight.

John was looking up at Jocelyn with the same tender and thankful face I had seen on the Rasta back there.

"What the hell's Rolf singing now?"
"Sounds like, "If today was a fish, I'd throw it back."
"You make any sense of him?"
"When I was waiting tables I wished more men were like him."
"You find him more attractive too?"
"Why d'you wanna know?"
"Someone with your looks could do a lot better than that piece of salt jerky."
"Must be why it's better for women to have looks than brains, 'cause most guys see better'n they think."

Chapter Fourteen

I snapped awake. John's small dark face bent over me. I could make out the white tape patches on one of his gaunt dark shoulders. I was in one of those deep sleeps, very deep, where it's painful to wake. First, I had to struggle to get my eyes open, then they snapped open and I looked to see if he held a knife. But he wouldn't have awakened me for that. ". . .other fellas. . ." I was missing half what he was saying. It was dark all around me. Bare flickers of yellow from the lit candle stub John held outlined the corrugated tin sheet that was the roof.

Disoriented, I panned the room. John moved in a slow limp back across the hut's floor. We were in Haitia Town, the sprawl of tiny shacks and huts through which we'd passed earlier. I remembered John pointing out the way, with Chancy carrying him – our trekking though the dripping darkening jungle to the shamble of huts where John lived.

John's woman, Esther, had fed us – handfuls of cold rice and beans we had gobbled down, in as shameless a way as I could think of, given how little John had to share. He had dug up, literally from a spot on the dirt floor, a can of sardines, from which we all took only one or two – John and Esther watching us the while, but not joining in our eating. I could not remember laying back on the dirt floor and falling asleep. But I recalled scraps of a dream.

I had gotten up in the night, left the others sleeping, had hiked down to the point across from where the Jamaicans were holed up with the hostages. At the water's edge I slipped in and began to swim. It was a grueling swim. I had to stop and float now and again on my back to rest. Salty waves slapped over my face.

The dark sky and stars had been so close...On board the ship, I talked the Captain into sending me back with a crew of SEALs to rescue the hostages. It was all so real, had made so much sense until I was awakened. I reached up to feel the salt water on my face, and found a film of sweat instead.

Outside I expected the night air to be cool, but it was not. It felt heated, simmering, even though it was dark. John led the way. He had blown out his candle, and I had to follow close. He made no noise. He took gingery steps, barely able to walk on his wrapped feet. We were nearly to the hut where Chancy and Rolf were bivouacked when I saw a silhouette seated on a log at the crest of a small rise. "Just a minute," I said to John. He went on to the hut.

I walked over to the log.

"You might as well go in, see what he's up to," Jocelyn said. It was too dark to see her face until I stepped around to the other side. Light from the half moon and stars showed her face, gave its smooth lines the sheen of burnished silver. The moon was the kind we called a broken one when I was a kid. The pale light brightened and dimmed across the smooth lines of her face and hair. She was staring off into the night.

"Couldn't sleep?" I asked.

Her head turned toward me, but she didn't speak.

"I had a hard time getting to sleep myself," I said. "I was trying to figure out what I'd done to tick the two of you women off. With Chancy I know I must've scooped him on a chance to be the hero. But there'll be other chances. What have I done, though, to irritate you and Monique?"

"It's not just you. There's no reason to take it

personally. It's all men at the moment."

"Like Mr. Randall?"

"He's certainly one of you." She nodded out toward the patch of water we could see from where we were, the ripples of waves stacking in rows of silver and black. "I don't doubt that as tough as the sea can be, and all the weather that goes with it, and all the nastiest creatures beneath its surface, that men don't pose an even greater hazard to the future of mankind, and to women in particular – not because we find men unfathonable, but because we don't suspect as often as we should that given the chance you'll always push us to the brink of survival with you, if only for the thrill of it, and you will."

"I can't see how any of us started all this trouble. That was the Jamaicans, unless you know more than we do."

"That wouldn't be so hard. There's a lot more to this than any of you know, or care to know. All I wanted to do was take care of people in the town, tend to animals, and stop some things that shouldn't have been going on anyway. It's nothing you strong-arms would give much of a hoot about."

"But, Monique," I said. "What put the chip on her shoulder about me?"

"She may just be used to a little more space than she's had since all this started. Her folks were killed when she was very young and she ended up living with an aunt and uncle who didn't much want her. She was quiet for a long time, learned to get along without anyone giving her any encouragement. But it's built up something of a deflector shield in her too. She's a little intolerant of people coming on to her. Maybe there's something about the uncle she's never even told me. It's just her. Don't let it bug you. At least she's not all in a lather all the time about trying to make everyone like her."

"You think I'm like that?"

She went back to looking out into the dark. "Oh, go on inside." She didn't turn to look at me. "Go ahead."

I left her and went over to the hut where John waited. He held the scrap of cloth that acted as a door to one side. Rolf and Chancy were huddled over the stub of a candle along the far wall of the hut. I half hoped they had something to eat. The other half of me was still embarrassed to the core by what we had taken of the little John had to eat.

I tried to remember how long we had been bouncing along in this disoriented fashion. It seemed weeks, though it could have only been a couple of days or so. I thought of Dot, wondered where she was, what she was doing, if she thought of me the tiniest bit. I could recall, with greater affection, the shower at Randall's place, the food.

I moved slowly, checking my bad leg. The knee was better than I expected. It was a bit swollen under the wrap, but I could flex it and put weight on it. I moved slowly over toward the light.

"How's the knee?"

"Functional. Why are we up?" I asked Chancy as I squatted beside him.

"We don't have all that much time."

"Are you thinking of trying Jocelyn's way in at this hour?"

"Nope. Too risky even if she was up to taking us through, which she's not now. She was acting like she'd help earlier, but that's all over now. We have to do something ourselves."

The flickering light gave a conspiratorial cast to our faces. Rolf and Chancy sat side by side facing me, both bent forward and were looking at me closely. "Have you thought of talking to her about what's bugging her.

Maybe. . . ."

"As fascinating as that line of thought might be," Chancy said, "We can't think about her. We need to focus on what needs to be done now."

That was Chancy in a nutshell. He could be as full of purpose as anyone I'd ever known, and it didn't have to be a right purpose, just one where he'd set his face and decided not to flinch. It wouldn't matter to him if he lost all the villagers in an effort to save a village. That sort of thing made him a climber in corporate circles, in a way I was starting to realize I could never be. I'd seen him charge into a meeting room with the same light in his eyes he had now.

Rolf said, "When Bahamian police finish up the fighting on the North end of the island, everyting lands on Dreadman. No tellin' about any hostages."

"What do you have in mind?" I watched Chancy. He had his small pack bundled and set to the side of the hut.

"What's holding Red Dreadman where he is?" he said.

"Why don't you just say it?"

"What's holding Dreadman where he is?" he repeated. I was not awake enough, and knew better to wrestle words with him when he was in one of his control moods.

"Okay. The cutter."

"Any chance of it going away," Chancy said, "or if it does, of rescuing any hostages then?"

Before I could respond, Chancy looked right at me and said, "We need to get them out of the fortress, someplace where they'll be spread out along a trail. But they'll stay holed up as long as those Rastas think they can make a dash for it with their boats."

"Good God. You want me to swim out to the cutter, talk them into taking it out of sight?" I was thinking back to my dream, parts of it were coming back more clear than before.

"They'd never go for that, not after how they treated us the first time they had us on board." Chancy glanced to Rolf. "We need to take out Dreadman's boats where they sit."

A sudden breeze from the sea swept over the top of the hut, rattled it. A cool draft swirled around inside the tiny room. John had squatted by the door. He watched us, listening, but not listening.

"You're sure Dreadman will leave then, won't just stay holed up in the fortress?"

"No sure ting, kid," Rolf said. He shrugged. "But he sure as tam hell is not so stupid enough to sit and wait. We all know what comes next."

"It's an odds-on bet," Chancy said, "but we have to take it. What I don't know about boats, Rolf here does."

"What do you have planned?" That feeling I had of stepping onto the soil of some other planet was growing a bit.

"There was a time back in New York City," Chancy said, "when I was living down in Chelsea, one of the locals, a fellow named Anthony, or Ant-Tony as he said it, slapped a small kid sitting on his stoop, told him to clear out, called him a 'little Jew boy.' Anthony had a blue Volkswagon beetle. That night someone took off the gas cap and put in a rag trailing out. They lit it. Next morning there were parts of that Volkswagon in the upper limbs of trees on Seventh and Eighth Avenues. Most of the neighborhood windows were shattered too."

"Won't Dreadman think to head in toward Randall's place, hole up there," I said. "It's the safest spot they'll probably think of, with plenty of supplies. It's what Randall thought earlier."

"That's exactly what we're counting on." The corner

of Chancy's mouth tugged with an upward twitch. "They'll be strung out along the trail on the way there. It'll give us a shot at freeing the hostages."

"And," Rolf help up the forefinger of his good hand, "Two tings these tam Rastas carry – money and guns, same as money. Tink of. . ."

Chancy interrupted. "That's not our focus, though." He was looking at Rolf.

I was thinking about the time out on the water when Rolf had hinted that I could toss Chancy overboard while he was out. That seemed a lifetime ago. They were sure tight now.

I hesitated, finally said. "We can't do that to Randall. Someone's got to warn him?"

"Why?" Chancy said. They were both staring at me.

"No matter what he does, or who he is, he deserves that."

"Don't go spineless on us." His eyes narrowed.

"I'm not."

"You think it shows more grit to be against us?" Chancy's eyes flicked to Rolf, then back to me.

"I'm not against you. I think we have to warn him. That's all."

"You sure you're not just trying to do what Jocelyn wants?"

Chancy had a point. Everything I did seemed to be for someone else, and not one of them had much appreciated it. My personal relations were going the way of my marriage, and perhaps for some of the same reasons. But I knew Chancy would do whatever he wanted, no matter what I said or felt. And, while he was not a forgiving person, he did sort through things in hindsight with more candor than most. Jocelyn had made a bigger and more valid impression on me, on top of which I was sick to my bones of shooting at people and killing them, no matter what is said of the mentality that settles on one during a war.

I looked right at him. "It's what I want."

"I wish you'd see your way to come with us. We could use you."

I did feel something inside like the tearing of a sheet. "Sorry to let you down."

"You have."

"No stomach for this kind of ting?" Rolf said. He and Chancy traded glances.

I was watching Chancy. He looked like someone else, someone I did not know as well as I thought I did.

"Yust tink," Rolf said, "Is like passing of your Wild West. Comes by yust once."

I dug into my pocket, came up with Chancy's lighter. I held it out to him. "You may be needing this."

I went back outside by myself. Jocelyn was where she had been, but was standing now. I went over to her, careful where I stepped in the dark. My night vision was nowhere near as good as John's.

"Well, what's it going to be?" she said. "Knives in your teeth and swinging on vines over the walls?"

I said, "I think he mentioned pulling the pins off grenades with our teeth, but he didn't say anything about any vines." She didn't laugh.

"You'll be right in there in the middle of it, right?"

"No. No I won't." I stood close to her, but could see no emotion on her face. The moonlight, like ice being chipped off a block, flickered in her eyes. It was a still night again, hot and with no more breeze. I could not remember a night when there was less wind. There was no rustle in the trees. "I'm going to head back to the estate, warn Randall that the posse might be coming his way."

Her head snapped to me. "You like Randall that much?"

"I didn't say I like him. But I think if Chancy gets his way the Rastas will be heading toward Randall's place, and I think one of us should let him know."

She hesitated. There was more she almost said, but didn't. Instead, she said, "Why don't you take Haitian John with you? You'll get lost for sure."

Soft steps were coming our way. It was Monique. I saw her hair coming before her tan face showed. When she was up to us she ignored me, asked Jocelyn, "What's up?"

"The fellows have a plan, one that should stir the hornets nest, probably drive Red in toward the estate." She nodded toward me. "He's off to warn Randall, and he's taking John. Do you want to go with them?"

"No, I'll stay here with you. You okay?"

"Fine. Just dandy."

"Why don't you try to get some rest."

"Sure. Why don't I do that? I'll do just that." Jocelyn walked slowly away from us. I did not get the impression she was going back to whatever hut they were in.

Monique turned to me. The exchange of information hadn't been all that subtle. But she was smiling now, and it looked as genuine in the moonlight as it was welcome to me. I felt relief that she felt more kindly toward me now than during the day, but wasn't sure if it didn't come from her thinking me some kind of harmless fool. Maybe she just suspected that I'd had to stand up to Chancy, and that pleased her. I wasn't sure, and my wits felt more like jello than sharp cold steel.

"Back there after she and Chancy were free from the Jamaicans," I said, "you mentioned something about her parents. What was that all about?"

"That was a long time ago, something personal."

"I'd really like to know."

She hesitated, then said, "Her family was in a boat accident – her parents, brother, and herself. Wind swept their sailboat up onto a reef, broke the boat in half. They were all injured, her parents the worst. Jocelyn didn't know enough to be able to help them. The tide was coming in and Jocelyn was the only one in a life jacket. She was able to hang onto her brother and save him, but both her parents died while she watched, just before another boat came along. It's what sent her into medicine. She swore a tougher Hippocrates' oath than most. Even when she ended up a vet, she still helps the natives and whoever she can, tries to do the right thing, even when it ain't the easiest. It's part of why I admire her so. That's all there is to it."

"Oh." But I was talking to myself. She had moved away as silently as she had come.

* * *

"Miss Doc Jocelyn sure be plenty up set. Yes she is."

Haitian John must have had the bones of a bird. I had been carrying him for a mile so far and could barely feel his weight on my back. The gun and small pack slung over one shoulder felt like they weighed more than John. My arms were tucked under his knees and his bony arms were around my neck. Dark as the trail was I caught glimpses of the white taped wrappings around his feet.

The dirt trail wound through the dense growth. It was somewhere nearer morning than the middle of night. But the night was black as anthracite here. The stars were hid by the overhanging trees and vines.

"No," John said, pointed with his right taped foot. "Dis other way der."

"She should be glad we're taking time to let Randall know what we're up to."

"Mistah Randall, he the las' man need be tole anythin'."

We were quiet for another quarter of a mile, John pointing the way and giving me an occasional nudge the way you'd steer a horse.

"John, I've learned something from all this."

"To stay to home, suh?"

"No." I chuckled, then sobered. "I don't know where home is anymore."

A few yards later, I said, "What brought you out here, John, to this particular island?"

"Boat."

"But why, I mean? Why did you end up here?"

"Was starvin', suh."

I hadn't figured John for any sense of humor, had to take what he said as the bones of literal truth.

"The first time I came here it was with Chancy, six or seven years ago. He'd stayed at Elbow Cay a few times, knew where to rent a boat, where to catch fish. I remember a time we went snorkel diving out on the flats of Tilloo Bank, in those rolling white sand dunes that form underwater there. We picked up starfish, conch, sand dollars. Later, what I remembered, when I got back home, was the taste of salt. I tried to recapture the feeling, even went to a natural food store, bought sea salt and mixed some in water. But sipping that wasn't the same as being down here. It wasn't the same at all."

"Dis goin' some place?"

"The trail or what I'm sayin'?"

"I know 'bout dis trail, suh."

We were quiet for the next mile or two. I began to sweat and feel John's weight more than I had. The knee was holding up, but once every dozen steps or so it gave a twinge – what still felt like metal parts rubbing the wrong way began to rend and shred.

We had a ways to go, and talking wasn't keeping my legs from going. I said, "It's like a woman. You may meet a dozen, half a dozen in your life who have the raw magnetic power to make you change, do things you might not otherwise do."

"Dat Esther mine. . ."

"What I'm struggling to say is that I realized that this island, this particular chunk of rock and plants, and the water around it, has that for me. Maybe a bit of it's being cut off from the rest of the world when I'm here. But it's the sound of the waves, the way the coconut trees sway and rustle in the wind, even the little tension between we tourists and the locals."

"I like it here too."

"As well you might," I said. One of the things about babbling to John, besides easing my own tension, was his only half listening or paying attention to what I said.

"We're not too far from it now, are we?"

"No. Not too far. You like Mistah Randall?"

"Not really," I admitted. Maybe he was wondering why I would go out of my way for the man. I was wondering a bit myself.

"You never said so 'fore."

"No. I believe it's a Haitian proverb that goes, 'Do not insult the mother alligator until you've crossed the river.

"Dat's good ad-vice, suh?" He waited a few more steps before he added, "You think you 'cross the river yet?"

* * *

The gate was closed when we got there. The sun was just coming up. No guards popped up to confront us. Just by looking at the signs he read on the path, John did not call out to anyone.

"Dat Mistah Randall, he comes and goes sometimes. He shut dis down a'fore."

"What we need is a bolt cutter to get through this fence," I said.

"Dis way."

I followed where John pointed. He had not left his sweaty perch on my back. Though he still felt as light as before, I was beginning to welcome a break from my role as beast of burden.

"Place back here where dey dogs dug a hole."

"Dogs?"

"Dey none of dem here no more. Prob'ly din get long with Mistah Randall's critters."

We came to the spot where a dog-sized furrow led under the chain link fence. Randall's men hadn't found it or filled it in. I lowered John. He crawled through. I followed. He climbed back on.

"Kind of quiet," I said. We came onto a path a hundred yards further that led around a truck garden to the buildings.

"Dass just it. Too quiet, suh."

It was a ghost town. All the buildings were locked and boarded. Randall and his men must have started closing down as soon as we were out of sight.

"Best gib it up," John suggested.

"Not just yet, John." I lowered him, let him walk gingerly on his taped feet. "One of these rocket scientists padlocked this warehouse door but left the hinge screws exposed. I hunted around for a small piece of metal I could use as a screwdriver, and came up with a rusty butter knife that would do fine. I began to unscrew the hinges. In minutes I had the door loose. I swung it open and went in. John followed with some reluctance.

The inside of the warehouse was empty. What few crates and cages had been left behind were empty, a few of them damaged or broken. The power had been turned off. We had only the morning light coming in through the leaning door to guide us. Beside me, John lit the stub of a candle he took from one of his pockets. By that light we went in to the back room, where Rolf, Chancy and I had stayed earlier.

All the cabinets here were locked. But with the same careful attention to detail as the outside lock. I eased to the floor and started in with the butter knife. Down there on the floor along the wooden floorboard, something else caught my eye. A telephone jack. It was empty, but I had not noticed it when we were here before.

John hung back. I got the cabinet open. A small flashlight was one of the first things I found. I flicked its switch and looked around, found bullion cubes, tea, a small can of stew, another of meat. Behind them I found something I welcomed more -- a telephone, an old black, beat-up dial model. But I hauled it out, moved over to the jack and plugged it in.

I thought about the power being off at the same time I recalled that these older phone jacks had batteries. I lifted the receiver and heard a dial tone. I began to dial a number I knew well. Getting the U.S. connection and giving my credit card number took a while, then I listened to a couple of rings before the phone was picked up.

"Myrna?" I said.

"I know who this is. Where's Chancy? From the news, all hell is going on there."

"You're not here?"

"One of your better questions. Didn't he share the note?"

"What note?"

"My note. I left you the one from Dot, put one in the bedroom for Chancy that was in much the same tone. What's going on down there? The news accounts are all garbled. But I've had the television unplugged for a day during the packing."

"You got out okay?"

"Way before any trouble started. Look, I'd like to chat, but there're a few things I need to . . ."

"You're. . .?"

"Leaving Chancy? I must say, you are razor-edge today. Surely you saw this coming, the same as with you and Dot. Look, the movers are at the door, so. . ." There was a click.

I hung up slowly, unplugged the phone and put it back in the cabinet. There was no one else I needed to call.

Where I had removed some of the cans on one shelf I spotted a small framed photograph on its side, the photo turned to the wall. I pulled it out. A crack ran across the glass, where it had been dropped. In the print, Randall and Dr. Jocelyn stood facing the camera. They smiled and each had an arm around the other. I could mention it to Chancy later, maybe. I put it back where I had found it.

The goods I had gathered from the cabinets were in a small pile. I looked up at John, who still hung back, looking at me. "You know where we can find any more, John?" I nodded toward what we had.

"None of dis my truck, suh."

"But we. . .you need. . ."

"Dem Jamaicans, dey loot, suh. Not me."

"Never? Not even in need?"

"I starve first. Esther too."

Well, that was that. I sat for a moment, staring in the dim candle light at the wrinkled skin of John's ankles above the white tape. His skin was like an elephant's. I shook myself. I picked up the supplies and put them back in the cabinet, even though they probably belonged to Jocelyn as much as Randall. I screwed the hinge screws back into place. I realized I still had the flashlight. I turned it off and lay it on the counter top. I could barely look John in the eye in the flickering light of his candle.

"Okay," I said. "Let's go." I believe I saw the glistening white flash of his teeth in a grin.

We were almost to the door when the first explosion shattered the quiet. It was far enough away to be at the cove where Dreadman kept his escape route boats. Another blast followed, and another.

John waited while I screwed the door back on. I turned and started to run toward the fence, looked back and saw John wincing with every step. I went back, turned, and he climbed up onto my back. I started to run, felt the gun banging against my back. I stopped, had John climb off, slipped the shoulder strap off and threw the gun over into the thick of some bougainvillea.

I like to think that I never at any point considered myself John's social or cultural superior, though I hadn't realized I might be his inferior. But, if he could be starving and not loot, then I could throw away a damned gun.

What I felt was a combination of shame and relief as the dark metal and wood of the gun whirled into the green and was lost from sight. It's what I should have done from the first, I told myself.

John climbed back on. I spun toward the fence and we were off to the races.

"Be careful with those crates."

"Welcome aboard, Mr. Randall. Please don't order the men around. They respond only according to rank."

"Thought you were going to nail those Rastas closer to home."

"They didn't cooperate."

"You sure that just isn't the way you wanted it?"

"You, of all people, know how unreliable they can be."

"Yeah. I guess you're right. There's nothing wrong with them that reasoning with the bastards wouldn't aggravate."

Chapter Fifteen

My load was lighter without the gun. John on my back was just there, part of me as I jogged through Randall's estate, past the truck farm, a small citrus grove, until we were at our hole in the fence. Explosions continued ahead. I glanced toward the sky where it was not obscured by the green limbs of trees. If smoke was lifting it was lost in the gray massing of cumulus clouds. The sky was stark and divided, the sun bright and harsh on one side, its blue as fragile as an egg shell. The other weather side, where we were headed, was a darkening ooze, with veins like a fresh hemorrhaging bruise.

At the fence I stopped, let John down. He started through the hole. "Things're going to be different next time," I was muttering as I crawled through, smelling the damp native soil as I did. "Very different."

I stood up on the other side, tottered. My eyes seemed to expand, contract their range. The leaves on the close bushes and trees were clear and distinct one moment, fuzzy and distant the next.

John started to climb back onto me. My arms went down to grab his bony legs and missed. I felt myself falling forward. I blacked out for what seemed only a moment or two. John was bent over me. I blinked up at him, started to rise but could only push myself up a few inches before flopping back to the ground. In the distance I heard what must have been the last of the explosions.

John hurried away as fast as his hurt feet would let him. He disappeared into the thick brush of the jungle on the outside of the fence. He came back, walking with careful mincing steps. He carried a gnarly, twisted half-sized breadfruit. The ones back in Randall's garden had been much larger, more perfect shaped. But parts of the one John held looked ripe.

He squatted on the ground beside me and brought the fruit down hard on his bony knee. It opened. He wrenched a large ripe chunk loose and handed it to me.

I chewed, not tasting anything, but knowing I needed food. I forced a swallow.

I wondered how much weight I had lost on this trip – one hell of a way to do it. I wouldn't recommend it as a spa to others. There was a point earlier when I had thought the whole experience was hardening me, making me tougher, more fit. But it had gone on too long. It was breaking me down now.

I ate and watched John eat. He gnawed at a tougher, more twisted piece of fruit than mine. It was a simple act, one that somehow epitomized his life. It was hard to tell if I was making sense to myself, if I wasn't hallucinating a tiny bit.

"I've heard that breadfruit is good for the heart," I said.

John continued to chew, shook his head that he didn't understand me.

I tapped the place on my chest over my heart, said, "High blood pressure, heart failure. The breadfruit. Good for that?"

His eyes got wide and worried.

"Forget it," I said.

I gnawed at the breadfruit, sucking at the rind, trying to get as much from it as I could. I felt as filleted as a fish, with about as much energy. "I wanted to be the good one, John. That's all. Is it so wrong to want to be liked, to be interesting? Do I seem the good one to you?"

"You okay so far, suh. I don' know none of y'all that

well."

I let the empty fruit rind fall from my fingers. This time when I pushed myself to my feet I was able to stand. The air around us seemed heavy, damp, and very still after the explosions had stopped. But that could have been the storm coming too.

I stood, waited for John to come climb onto my back. He stood and came around to face me. "You okay, suh?" I nodded. The whites of his eyes around the large brown irises were stained a light muddy brown. A ridge, like scar tissue, was raised in a half moon along the inside of each iris. He looked tired, worried, as sad as the whole history of mankind in the world. As different as his eyes were from mine, they held what I would expect to see in my own if I could look.

"Climb on," I sighed.

He did, slowly, like a mahout mounting an old and tired elephant.

I moved my resisting legs and started down the trail.

At first my steps were deliberate, careful. I knew we would get there eventually. I heard the first of shots being fired. There was a machine burst of answering shots. I forced my feet and aching knee to go faster.

"John," I said as I shuffled into what I thought was a jog, "I've been trying to think back to when life was simple. People were born, lived day to day, were hunter/gatherers, died when it was their turn. I picture someone living on an island like this, off coconuts maybe, fish, I don't know. But the life is simple, good. Am I talking too much. I do prattle on sometimes. . .when I'm. . .tense, you know. A trainer from a gym told me once that the best exercise you can do is when you can still talk as you move."

"Don' do no ex-or-cize, suh."

"The past few days have been such a blur to me, John, that I'm pressed hard to make any sense of it all. Even with all the terrible things that have happened it's not that much different from my life before now. I've just been rolling along, day to day, in much the same funk of a blur – an ostrich with my head in the sand."

John didn't say anything. He was being more obvious about steering me, giving me solid nudges with his feet. But I didn't mind or care. It was a boon not to have to think about the trail, about remembering which way we had come. As bright as it still was, I could see the trail. I knew most of the route back and let John's nudges do the rest.

"My wife left me, John. Did you know that?"

"No, suh."

"Just one of the things this week. I've killed people, which is bigger. It's something I never thought I would, or could do. I'm not too proud of it. But all I can feel about any of it is some hollow lack of feeling. Shock maybe. It's not even been the wake-up call I may have needed, craved. Well, all that's over. My eyes are opening now. What I had with Dot is over. Whatever intimacy I was faking, whatever distance I let creep in, all that's past. I have to take the rap for it, know there's nothing fixable there, no more than I can get back the stuff of mine that was trashed or lost on this trip."

"Hmmm." John nudged me to the right fork in the path.

"But I can re-evaluate, figure out what does matter, and move on with that. Do you have any children, John?"

"Two son. One Haiti, other in U.S."

"Are you glad you had them?"

"Suh?"

"Are they a comfort to you?"

"They not heah, suh."

"What do you think of Monique?"

"Suh?"

"Does she seem like a nice person, a good person to you?"

"Suh?"

"I've been a fool." I had to reach to recall what Dot looked like, but I could remember every detail of Monique – the brown of her eyes, the soft down on her tanned arms, even the mole below her right eye. . .especially the mole. "Maybe I'm just tired, worn to the bone, hallucinating." The very best thing about Monique was the way she could be frowning one moment and then burst into a smile. Was it the contrast? Could it be as simple as that?

"In truth, I know very little about Monique. But what did I know about Dot? About myself?"

I felt John shifting on my back, uncomfortable, or wary the way a rider gets on a horse that may be getting ready to bolt.

"With Dot there was passion, at first. A lot of it. There was friendship too. She was my best friend. But now, there's nothing. What is there about Monique that makes me think that it could be different with her?"

We could hear the shooting getting louder before we were close enough to see what was going on. A rustle on the path ahead should have made me cautious. But I was running numb. A man and boy burst around a bend, running toward us.

"Mistah Jules," John said.

I staggered to a stop. They did not stop, only pushed around us and kept running. "John," the man said. Then they were out of sight.

"Hostages?" I said.

"Prob'ly."

I turned back up the trail and started toward the gunfire. After being held for a couple of days by a Jamaican weapons trafficking gang I might have lost the edge off some of my social graces as well.

A few more yards up the trail we came to a middle-aged woman crouched in the center of the path, panting before she could go on. The shots seemed very close now.

"All the hostages get free?" I asked.

She looked up at me with a start, gave John a double-take until she recognized him.

"Most I could tell about," she said. "I'm waitin' to see if Jesse made it loose. Bless those fellas what sprung us. Which way you fellas goin'?"

"That way." I nodded toward the shooting.

"I'd recommend against it," she said.

When we started off in that direction anyway, she added, "Say thanks to them what rescued us if you'd be so kind."

I followed the trail, but moved with renewed caution. We could hear shouting, guns firing from more than one direction. We got close enough to hear a bullet snip off leaves behind us. I stopped on the path. John got off. It was not a good time to stick up high.

The trail sloped upward ahead of us. Thick vegetation made it harder to see what was happening. A burst of automatic weapon shots rattled in echoes through the trees, their sound bouncing off the leaves, making the direction of the firing hard to pinpoint.

I got as low to the trail as I could and crawled forward. John was right behind me.

Feeling along the path on my hands and knees, I was tired, maybe dazed, half-aware. But I was angry. At the sound of every shot I was thinking about these guns.

Where did they come from. The AK-47 I had tossed away was made by the Russians. The uzi Chancy had been using was made in Israel. I'd seen plenty of guns made in the States, as well as Sig Sauers from Germany, Italian Berettas, Austrian Glocks. There were Brazilian, Swiss, Spanish, Danish guns. Every country had its people getting rich making these things. I don't know what this stuff was doing crowding my head right now, shots from some Jamaican posse buzzing over my head like metals bees. I hoped I wasn't just feeling sanctimonious, my gun laying back in the bushes somewhere at Randall's place.

A row of dirt flew upward in the path in front of my face. A furrow marked where a stray bullet had entered. I moved faster, hugged a side of the path that took me closer to the bole of a tree. I peeked around, could see the backs of three men wearing bright colors. Two of them had the floppy multi-colored hats. The third man looked like a native who had joined their ranks. He wore a shirt I'd seen in some of the tourist shops. A cartoon Reggae skull of a face, wearing a Jamaican cap and sporting dreadlocks, leered out like a skull and crossbones. In Jamaican colors, the lettering on the shirt said, "Fear this!"

They fired up at a clump of trees at the top of the path. A head shot out from behind one of the trees. A burst of shots sprayed the area and sent the men ducking. The head was Chancy's. I was too far away to see any gleam in his eye, joy at the fray. But I could imagine it. Man, he had to be eating this up.

Footsteps came tearing up the path behind me. I shuffled as fast as I could into a thick stand of bushes, made room for John beside me. Some of the posse hurried past, seeking to get around to the far side of the spot where I'd seen Chancy, to flank them. If it was me, and I'd just lost all my hostages in some surprise confusion, I would have gone on to Randall's place and holed up. But whatever had happened must have put them into a rage. That or they needed new hostages. Either way, this posse, or what remained of it, seemed intent on getting at whoever was up there.

In spite of all the noise of shooting and shouting, either John or I made a noise that spun the head of one of them toward us. He shouted. A couple of the others turned back toward us. Chancy's head popped out high on the hill, and he let off a couple of shots. Monique stood up beside him. Her shots all went high. They were as trapped as we were. Men were all around us. I felt John pressing against my back.

The closest of the Rastas was coming back our way. He was near enough for me to see his bloodshot eyes. The other two had turned around and were edging and circling closer. A shot or two snipped through the leaves at us. One ricocheted off the tree's trunk.

Past the shoulder of the Jamaican nearest us, I saw movement behind a tree. It was Jocelyn peering out low to the ground from where she had been hiding. She was as far down on the hill as John and I were. But she was behind the men coming at us. She held one of the guns clenched in both hands. I saw her eyes click on John and me, register surprise. Her eyes opened like the twin barrels of a gun, the two silver eyes pointing as hard toward me as bullets when the trigger has been pulled.

In that second I could read in her look what I should have sensed before ever setting out toward Randall's – that she knew the place would be abandonded. She's sent us to get us out of harm's way, and here we were back again. She did not look happy about it.

She pulled herself farther out from the tree bole, dragged herself, and that seemed a strain. In her extended arms I could see she clutched one of the fallen AK-47s. The barrel of the gun lifted, flames spouted, and I heard the chatter of the shots as the Jamacian nearest us spun and dropped.

The other two wheeled in her direction, firing as they turned. I watched one of them tumble forward, clutching his middle. Leaves and dirt sprayed all around the base of the tree where the other one was firing. In the blur of shots coming from both directions it was hard to follow what was happening. Through a clear spot in the smoke I could see Jocelyn's face, the shots seemed to be missing her. The last Jamacian stopped firing, stared at her. I may have imagined it, my ears were still ringing from the shots, but I though I heard him say, "Randall."

Jocelyn's eyes had narrowed to slits. She squeezed at the trigger in a sustained rattle of shots until her gun clicked on empty. She kept squeezing.

A couple more shots came from the Jamaican. His gun had lifted, and his shots went high and wild, snipping off leaves in the trees. He fell over onto his side.

In the relative silence that followed, with shots coming farther up the hill, I watched Jocelyn squeezing away at the gun as if trying to wring out ammo that was not there. John and I were huddled so close together that any one of the Jamaicans who got close to us could have finished both of us off with one shot.

I shook myself, pushed up from the ground and stood. There was no one else near us. In the distance we could see the backs of the other Jamaicans still climbing far up the hill and pushing closer to the others.

John eased to his feet beside me. I felt him put his hands on my shoulders from the back. I reached down to hold his legs. When he was on, I moved as quick and quiet through the low brush as I could, glancing down at the bodies of the fallen men to make sure they were finished. Startled eyes stared up from one of them, but they were not seeing anything. The others were as dead.

Up close I could see that Jocelyn had not moved. Her arms clenched the gun and she still pointed it and pulled the trigger of the empty weapon. Her eyes were almost shut, and one tear ran down like a wet scar through the dust that covered her face.

I came around the tree and eased John to the ground. She didn't turn to look at us, though she had seen us. I moved to her, put a hand on her shoulder. She rolled over onto her back. The gun fell from her open fingers with a soft thud onto the mashed and bullet- scarred vegetation.

Her eyes swept over John and I. On the lower left side of the front of her shirt there was a wide wet red ring of blood, darker and black at its center. "You're hurt," I said.

Her eyes blinked. Her teeth pulled at her left lower lip. "I. . .I. . ."

The wound was not fresh. It had not happened in the last flurry we had witnessed. I bent closer. Shots still came from up the hill.

She had to take a deep breath, struggled to speak. "I'll never forgive that son-of-a-bitch for making me kill people."

"What have you got there, Sidney?"
"Couple of reels, Mr. Randall?"
"Pretty nice Penns. How'd you come by them?"
"Fella was here left them behind."
"Well, get rid of them."
"Are you. . ."
"Throw them out, bury them, toss them over the side. I don't care. I don't want any traces."
"What about Doc Jocelyn?"
"The hell with Doc Jocelyn."

Island - Russ Hall

Chapter Sixteen

I looked around, saw Jocelyn's black medical pack. It lay half under a small bush where she had dragged it when she had crawled behind the tree. I was going to wave John over toward it, then thought of his wrapped feet.

I scurried over to it. Sharp rocks and twigs poked at my palms and knees. I brought it back. John had bent and was brushing her hair back from her face. She started to wave his hand away, thinking it was me perhaps. She saw me coming back to her with the bag. "Got to help the others," she said.

"We will." I had the pack open and was digging through it. I spread a row of clean wide leaves on the ground beside her and began to lay out some of the things I would need.

"Give me that," she said. I handed over the bag. John stood watching the thick matted green around us.

I nodded back to where the Jamaicans had fallen. "Guns," I mouthed. Jocelyn lay on her back, digging into her pack. All of her attention was focused on that. John nodded, began to step away gingerly on his padded feet.

She pulled out a syringe and a small brown plastic vial. "You know how to administer this?" she said. Before I could answer, she began to tear the wrapper off the syringe herself.

She still lay on her back. I tugged the bottom of her t-shirt out of her jeans. She winced, but did not stop me. She pushed the syringe into the vial and measured out a small dose of what looked like morphine.

I lifted the bottom of her shirt, used both hands to work it clear until her torso was exposed all the way to the underside of her left breast. As she lifted her left arm to push the needle in, the smooth white flesh of the breast slid into view, all the way to the pink brown of the areola. I looked down to the wound, tugged the edge of the shirt back down until I could only see the hurt area. The wound was a pouting red hole with blood drying to a near black on the proud flesh around the wound. I tore off a wide strip from the bottom of my shirt, lifted her at the hip to slip a cloth under her. The exit wound was larger, but not huge – probably a steel-jacketed shell. The blood had coagulated on both sides. It was no longer flowing, though both sides had a shine from new blood as the wounds oozed.

"You're of hardy stock," I said. "I'm surprised you're not in shock." Getting hit by an automatic weapon's bullet has sent large men into shock before, more often than not.

"After what we've been through," she said through clenched teeth. "What could shock any of *us*?" After the last word, a wave of calm swept over her – the morphine kicking in.

John came back carrying two of the guns, along with their ammo belts. One was an uzi, the other was one of the AK-47s. Jocelyn saw what he was carrying, but was occupied by the first wave of the morphine. She gave a small smirk that stayed on her face for only a second. "Don't worry about me. The others. Take. . ." she was floating.

"There'll be time. You'll be more help to us patched."

John nodded up the hill where we could both see that the distant Rastas had halted and were firing but not advancing. A steady pace of shots came from the top of the hill, keeping the Jamaicans from any hasty ideas. "Dem Jamaicans, mon, dey don' expect dat. No dey don'."

I lifted a piece of gauze to my mouth to lick it. Jocelyn said, "Don't."

I stopped.

"There are all manner of germs in saliva," she said.

"There's no water."

She sighed. Her eyes closed slowly, then snapped open. "Use urine."

"What?"

"It's sterile and the uric acid can even help a wound," she said. "And when you clean the wound, swipe outward, not inward."

I stayed low, but moved away, unable to obtain the necessary liquid so close to her. My water bottle was empty. I used that.

John gave me one raised dark eyebrow when I scuttled back like a crab. My knee gave a twinge, but there was no time to pay attention to that. Steady shots back and forth came from up on the hill.

John bent low and watched me swab the wound. I reached for the antiseptic.

"You can put that away," Jocelyn said. There was a bit of slur to her words. "It's no good for a deep wound."

For some reason I thought of a western or some war film where the wounded man opens a cartridge and pours the gunpowder onto the open bullet wound, then lights it. Whatever her half-closed eyes saw in mine brought a frown. But that eased as I worked. I was more efficient than she may have expected.

When I had the wound clean I used butterfly sutures to close the entrance wound, then gauze and tape to hold that in place.

She faded in and out in the early stages of the morphine. In a lucid moment she said, "You do this quite well. Have you been to war before?"

Her question was punctuated by two shots above us. I watched her face. It was not flush. "Don't try to talk."

I eased her to her side and from there to her stomach. There was some dirt in the larger exit wound, which took some harder rubbing to get out. She winced, called out, "Watch it." The shot that hit her had been made from a distance. There was no powder around the entrance wound. But she must have been standing with her back against a tree when it she was hit. The metal jacket of the bullet had shattered and fragments had bounced back to make smaller frag wounds. Bits of bark were also embedded near the wound. I cleaned each of the smaller wounds and dressed them. I used the longer SteriStrips to suture the exit wound before dressing and taping it. This side took longer.

"Deys movin' agin," John said softly.

I looked up the hill and could see nothing, save a bush twitch now and then.

"We'd better get moving to help them," Jocelyn said. Her voice was clearer and firmer. She had either adjusted to the morphine or it had run some of its course.

"Just a bit more cleaning and taping to do," I said. "There are still some things that can't be fixed with duct tape, and this is one of them."

"Monique. . ."

"I know she's up there," I said. "So's my friend Chancy."

"You say he's your friend. How do you know?" She was pressing her abdomen with her hands. She reached around to feel at her back where there was no wound.

"What are you doing?"

"Feeling for any tenderness or swelling that shouldn't be there. I think the bullet went through without any major damage to organs. But I want to watch for hemorrhaging."

"How do I know what?" I said.

"That he's your friend. You two act strange for friends."

"We do at that," I said. I was keeping my voice low.

Before I could have explored or explained my loyalty to Chancy I would have needed to understand it far better than I did at the moment.

"Tell me one thing." Her voice was little more than a string of breaths.

"What?" I had only a strip of tape or two to go.

"Your name. You never said, and Chancy never calls you by it."

"I've asked him not to."

"You see. There's one thing he gives you. He honors a request like that, however stupid."

"It's Dave," I said. "Dave Jones. Actually, most people call me Davey."

"Ah, I get it now. Davey Jones. You certainly couldn't ever go on the sea with a name like that."

"I know. It's not that big of a deal. My being uptight about it made it bigger."

"You're less of a prig some times than others," she said.

"You're all done," I said. "Ready to go?"

She tugged her shirt down over the wrappings, started to sit upright, had to lay back and hold out a hand. I lifted her to a sitting position. John came closer, wincing on his feet but walking on his wrappings. He bent to help her to a standing position.

I got the medical things back in the bag, shoved some AK-47 rounds from one of the belts into the gun Jocelyn had emptied. I rose and handed each of them a gun.

John did not seem to know how to handle his, but found the extended butt handy as a short crutch. He slipped Jocelyn's black pack over his shoulder. Jocelyn frowned, but took the uzi I gave her.

She stumbled taking her first step, fell against me. I put an arm around her and lifted, careful not to press against her wounds. She shifted the gun to her left hand and put an arm over my shoulder. John was very slow, and fell behind. His feet hurt him a lot. But he didn't complain.

We took soft steps, swinging to the far side from where we had last seen the Rastas creeping up the hill toward the others. We had to stop every few feet to let her rest, and for John to catch up.

"Davey," she said, was close enough to breath a chuckling whisper into my ear. "Davey Jones. You're a bit of a slow egg to boil, aren't you?"

"I am at that," I whispered back, motioned for her to be quiet. We were getting closer. John nodded to a spot in the thick green ahead of us. I had seen the leaves rustle too.

Jocelyn leaned very close, pressed her mouth to my ear. "It all comes down to this." Her words were barely discernable. It sounded like those of my conscience. "You give, and see what you get in return. You don't always get what you expect. But that shouldn't sour you on giving. Sometimes you even compromise your principles. Sometimes, more rarely, you get back more than you gave."

I wiggled my gun back and forth in front of her to tell her no more talking. I moved my arm off her and motioned for John and her to get low and stay put. The Rastas ahead of us had their attention toward the top of the hill. But they might look back, expecting the three we had left back there to catch up.

Above us, the sun shone through small gaps in the thick green growth making yellow sparkles. The day was heading toward late afternoon and the jungle around us was muggy and warm enough to bake bread. I had been hungry so long I felt light-headed. But I was able to crouch low and crawl forward.

I had in mind a simple flanking maneuver. It was hard to say how many of the crew there had been in the first place, or how many were left. But if they were in the least organized, they would be spread in a circle around the hill. I crawled toward where we had seen rustling leaves. I stopped to pick a thorn out of my left palm. Ahead of me, bright colors of a shirt showed suddenly as a man rose to fire up at movement on the hill. Two single shots answered. They had switched from automatic. Ammo must be running low up there.

I thumbed the selector switch on my gun to single and slid forward across stickers and leaves that rustled more than I would have liked. I waited to move until shots sounded to cover as much of my noise as possible. A few yards farther up the hill, I could make out the shirt of the man who had fired. His back was to me. I slithered closer until I could see him clearly. But I could not bring myself to plug him in the back.

I looked around for a stone. None was handy. A hermit crab crawled out from under a young coconut brush beside me. It had a black and white screw shell on its back. I grabbed for it and got it before it could sidestep out of reach. There was enough heft to the shell. The legs continued to move and the pinchers grab at air. I threw it toward the crouched Jamaican and hit him high on the back of his neck.

He whirled and stood. I was lined up on him. While his gun was still raising I hit him square in the chest. That was as close to the line of sporting as I could get.

Five yards to the right of him another Rasta stood, already firing. A burst of shots ripped at leaves and brush in a sweeping line toward me. I swung my barrel toward him and fired three times, one of the shots catching him above his left eye. He slammed backward.

Two spaced shots came from the hill, banging into the tree beside me and plowing a furrow in the dirt between my spread legs. There was no time to ponder the irony of getting this close only to be finished off by the ones I sought to save. I dove behind the tree as three more shots sliced the air where I had stood.

I waited to the count of twenty and began to crawl up the hill, my gun across my arms in imitation of war films. From tree to tree I moved upward, swinging by the fallen Jamaicans to take their ammo belts. Seeing them close and dead did not move my stomach this time, whether that was from its being so empty I could not say. I tried not to rustle the bushes or make a target out of my movements. But a stray shot now and again came very close. When I was close as I could get without getting plugged, I shouted a whisper, "Chance."

Shots came from the far side of the hill. But it was quiet around me, except for the screech of a bird that had landed in the tree tops and taken off again.

"It's me," I tried again, louder.

A head popped up out of the brush within feet of me. It was Chancy. "Christ you came close to getting it," he said. "I was sure I was about to get one or two of the bloody blighters on this side."

"There aren't any bloody blighters on this side," I snapped. "I just took care of that. Get the others and come on."

He moved closer until he could whisper. "You're going to have to help," he said. "What about. . .?"

"Jocelyn and Haitian John are down the hill. We've got to move."

He waved an arm toward the top of the hill and turned and started up. I had to follow.

The top opened into a small clearing. Someone had piled fallen logs, limbs, and coconuts into a semicircle. It was the Battle of Bunker Hill all over again. Rolf sat on the dirt with his back to the pile. An automatic weapon lay at his side with its breech open – out of ammo. He had Monique clutched to his chest and his hand was pressed to her mouth. Her eyes were wild and hysterical.

Chancy rushed to the makeshift bunker and fired single shots in three systematic directions. Then he dropped low as shots came back at them. He saw the ammo belts I carried and waggled a hand at me. I tossed him the belts. He busied himself loading his and Rolf's guns, cursing quietly when the ammo in one of the belts didn't match.

Rolf had a strip of cloth tied around his head. A trickle of wet red ran down from its side. His eyes swung toward me slowly, finally clicked. Concussion, at the least.

"Just grazed him," Chancy said. He finished loading the guns. "She took one in the leg."

There was a bloody smear on her hip, high and above the line where her shorts fell. From the way her leg lay, the bone was at least clipped, maybe broken. Oh, we were a fine mess of marines we were.

Chancy heard something, jumped to his feet and moved to the wall, rose and fired. He dropped back down and looked at me. A smear of black was across one cheek. Other than that, he seemed in top form. He said, "What the hell kept you, anyway?"

MARSH HARBOUR, Bahamas – *Jerome Randall, longtime resident of Elbow Cay, Abaco Islands, was lost at sea in a boating mishap Thursday, unrelated to the troubles on the island. The incident occurred in moderate seas while Mr. Randall was a passenger on a U.S. Coast Guard vessel.*

Special Agent Ross Cureen, of the ATF, said the loss is unfortunate since Mr. Randall was being very helpful in clearing up recent weapons trafficking in the Caribbean arena. The accident is being investigated, but there is little suspicion of a suicide or foul play. The loss is regretted by all who knew Mr. Randall here in the Bahamas.

Chapter Seventeen

An occasional shot sounded behind us, each like a question mark. The shots were muffled by trees and the rising humidity as we moved farther away. We made good time heading down the slope. The Rastas would wonder soon enough why there were no answering shots from the hill.

Rolf held a hand over Monique's mouth and supported her upper body. I cradled her from the waist down, her one leg dangling at an angle. She screamed into Rolf's palm when her leg swung the wrong way. Getting Monique down the hill was awkward, but it gave Rolf something to hang onto. He came and went on us. One minute he would be sharp and aware, the next his eyes would glaze and he made a low soft noise, "Tam, tam, tam, tam, tam, tam. . ." He sounded like a steam boat, or lawn mower. It was not enough noise to give us away unless someone was very close. But it unnerved me more that the crack of a twig stepped on, or the loud screech of the startled birds that flew from our path.

The trail opened and there was Haitian John. He sat cross-legged beside Jocelyn. She lay on her back with her eyes closed. John's mouth stretched wide and lifted at the corners. His teeth showed white as the Cheshire cat's. Our stopping coincided with one of Rolf's clear moments. His smile matched John's.

"I'm glad to see some of us are enjoying ourselves," Chancy said.

Jocelyn's eyes snapped open. She made a groggy try at sitting upright. Her head thumped back to the dirt. Her hair was in a tangle and held bits of leaves. But it didn't seem to bother her. "Mon. . .? Monique?" Her eyes stayed open.

Rolf and I lowered Monique beside Jocelyn. It seemed to calm Monique – that or not being carried any further. She did not yell.

I got the medicine pack from John and carried it to Jocelyn. I put a hand under her shoulders and helped her sit upright.

"Her leg," I said.

She glanced at the leg. "Bring me four or five sturdy sticks about a foot long, and some twine. I don't want to use up all the tape."

It took me a minute or two to find and trim the sticks. As I came back I saw Jocelyn putting away the brown plastic vial. She put the syringe she'd used back into its wrapper and put it back into the pack. Monique lay looking up through the trees at the flecks of yellow sun dancing through the leaves. She smiled. It was the first smile I had seen from her in a while.

Whatever flitting attraction I had for her earlier was gone. I could not say what had killed the spark. Perhaps I had new values, as much admiration for Jocelyn's motives as caution about Chancy's.

Jocelyn worked on Monique's leg. Haitian John watched. Chancy was on a self-imposed patrol. I went over and stood in one place while he paced back and forth along the edge of the clearing. Rolf sat at one end of the circuit. He was midstream in one of his catatonic spells. He made a different low purring sound now: "Geez, tam, tam, tam. Geez, tam, tam, tam." The steamboat had changed gears, or something. I looked in the direction where Chancy was staring and could see no movement.

"Jocelyn," I said. "You think you should take a look at Rolf?"

Chancy squinted a look at me, but said nothing.

"Bring him this way."

It was quiet around us. The last of the distant shots had stopped. The wind made a flutter among the high fronds of the coconut trees. The fragments of sky that showed through the tree tops were pale blue boiled paler by the sun. I could hear waves smash against rocks not all that far from us. We were closer to the Atlantic side of the island than I had thought.

I tapped Rolf on the shoulder. He looked up at me, his eyes bright and clear in the folds of his red face. He was back amongst us. "Is Rolf's turn?" he asked.

I helped him to his feet, could barely do it with him helping. It made me glad he was not one of us who needed to be carried.

We tottered to Jocelyn. She waved Rolf down beside her. She had caught some of Chancy's sense of urgency. Our not hearing shots was the loudest sound we heard. She finished tying and taping Monique's hip splint in place and turned to Rolf. She reached for the torn strip of shirt, now soaked in blood and sweat, and began to unwind it from his head.

"A little off sides," he said. "Not too much off top." He gave me an over-elaborate wink.

Chancy waved me back over. I went that way.

"They about done?"

"Yeah."

"Any bright ideas, old boy?" I couldn't tell if his eyes were just tired or apologetic.

I looked up through the trees in the direction of the sound of waves. "Just one," I said. I pointed up.

Chancy's eyes tracked to the East. "Geez-us damn," he said, low and quiet, and with none of Rolf's spin on it.

High in a sliver of sky that showed between two of the

taller palms, bouncing in a sea breeze on its cord, was the balloon the Coast Guard sailors had tied to our boat about seven lifetimes ago.

Across the clearing, Jocelyn put the last piece of tape on Rolf's new headdress. "What now?" she said.

"This way," Chancy said. He pointed. "We head East."

* * *

Haitian John was on my back. Rolf carried Monique cradled in his arms. The wrapping around Rolf's head was whiter and cleaner than that around his left hand. Chancy carried Jocelyn on his back. It was hard for me to tell which of them felt more uncomfortable about the arrangement.

Chancy kept turning to look behind us. He carried a gun in each hand. Jocelyn said to him, "Don't seem so disappointed we didn't get more of an encounter than we did. These Jamaicans can track, and I doubt that you have done much to endear yourself to them."

I turned back to the trail when I heard a thud. Rolf had bumped into a coconut trunk that bent into the path. He shifted to a low, "Geez, geez tam, geez, geez tam, geez, geez tam." The steamboat seemed to sputter. Monique's eyes were closed and she still smiled. Jocelyn must have given her a pretty good jolt.

A hole appeared in the tree beside Rolf's head at the same time I heard a shot. I rushed forward and tugged Rolf forward into a thicker cluster of trees. I heard a flurry of shots.

"Scramble people," Chancy shouted. We had already scrambled and continued to scramble. Rolf and I were rushing forward with our loads. I glanced back and saw

Chancy turn and shoot back into the brush with both hands. Jocelyn had the uzi. She was still on Chancy's back, but firing.

My bad knee was grinding and it was a struggle to take each step. And we hadn't eaten. I was surprised I was able to move at all. The bullets coming at us helped. Still, there was a purity to the moment, some of it perhaps from having a light head from lack of food. Each detail of the leaves we passed stood out in stark detail.

With that clarity I burst through the wide leaves of a sea grape bush and stood looking at the Atlantic Ocean. Rolf stood on the lava and rock skirt and watched foamy waves burst into upward sprays on the hard black rock that lined the shore in a three-foot cliff. The boat, with the line still climbing into the sky to the balloon, rocked on its side along the rock, banging into the shore with each wave. But it still floated. Water filled the inside up to the gunwales. Waves splashed in from the ocean side.

Where the hull was smashing against the rocks, holes had been stoved into the boat's side. I stood and stared. John stayed perched on my back, said nothing.

Rolf eased Monique to the ground. Her eyes were open and she was looking around. "What can I do to. . . ," she said. Rolf was coming back from the thick green of the vegetation at the water's edge. ". . . help?" she finished. He carried an armload of coconuts. Shots were being fired far back along the path we had come. There was no pattern to them.

"Food?" I asked.

"For hull." He dropped his load, turned and hurried back to the jungle.

I eased John down and went to gather coconuts.

We had a pile of them heaped in a few minutes. Rolf stood for a second looking at the boat.

"Welcome back," I said.

"Get on boat, by geez-tam Hesperus, and get line back to Rolf."

"What line?"

"Balloon."

I eased down across the sharp lava points and huge rocks made black by the crash of waves. Up close, the boat's banging against the rocks made a hollow, "Boom. Boom. Boom." Back in the dense green, a bullet ricochetted off a rock or trunk of a tree.

Every third or fourth wave, the boat was tugged out farther, then slammed close again with the following set of waves. Out across the Atlantic, the water looked dark blue, with white caps on the four to five foot waves. High cirrus clouds swept in horse-tail streaks across one patch of the sky, high above the cool breeze pushing along the shore. The rest of the sky was clear.

The boat pitched and yawled like a bronco in a chute. Even when it was banging against the rocks, it was a good leap across a distance that changed with every wave.

"Go," Rolf said. He held bits of loose coconut fiber in his palm. He let them drop. As they dropped, the breeze tugged the strands in a line parallel to the shore. "Goot. If we can get away from rock. . ."

The boat was moving along the shoreline a few inches each time it hit. I leaped and missed the bobbing side of the boat, fell into the very cold water over my head. A spray of underwater bubbles surrounded me as I dropped. Sharp rocks were beneath me. I kicked upward. I bobbed to the surface, gasping and tasting salt. The shock of impact and the cold was replaced by seeing the boat rush toward the black rocks behind me. I scrambled, pulling myself hard as I could along the side of the boat until I was at the stern just as it slammed.

I climbed up the side of the motor and pulled myself on board, almost stepping on the bait knife as I did. The water inside was nearly to my waist.

I reached for the bait knife. It skittered across the deck underwater like a bar of soap. When I had it, I pulled at the cord tied to the balloon until the balloon was within reach. I cut the cord, watched the balloon pop upward and be swept along and slightly away from the shore. Nothing small and heavy was loose to tie to the line. I sloshed to the seat behind the console, dug in the submerged bag on the seat, found the camera. It was a soggy hard lump inside the case. I didn't even want to open the case and look at it. I tied one end to the cord, threw that toward the shore.

"Tie thicker rope," he shouted.

I had already started to the bow. I reached underwater and tugged the hatch open, pulled out the spare anchor rope. It was thick enough. I untied the cord from the balloon and made a clove hitch knot on the end of the thicker rope. I cleated off the thick rope on the side closest to shore.

Rolf and Haitian John stood side-by-side. They pulled in the string and then the rope. They hauled at the rope until the boat moved closer to the shore, finally snugged up against it. Rolf tied the rope hard enough around a rock to keep it from banging. The boat tilted toward shore, which made it easier for them to get on board.

Haitian John was throwing coconuts over into the boat. He and Rolf had cut some in half with the machete. I thought I had seen Rolf chewing something. I grabbed at one of the halves that had a flash of white inside. I used the bait knife to pry out a thick chunk. I put the whole thing in my mouth and chewed. I had never had a steak that tasted better.

Rolf was carrying Monique. "You want to help," he was saying. "We need to bail out boat."

I stood up on the flat of the bow to reach out and bring her on board. I lowered her so she could sit. Water swept over the wrapping Jocelyn had put around Monique's thigh. If the salt stung at all, she did not let on. I had found the bailing scoop from earlier. I handed her that. She started bailing as fast as she could.

Haitian John and Rolf clambered on board. John took a coconut half in each hand and began to bail. Rolf used his good hand to bail. I had Chancy's empty cigar container and one of the coconut halves. We all bent our backs to it.

"Better go over side," Rolf said. "Push coconuts into holes."

"That fix it?"

"Can't hurt."

I climbed over onto the shore and from there eased down into the crashing waves. All of the holes were along the shore side of the boat. Rolf dropped coconuts to me from inside the boat. Some of the coconuts went in easily. Some I had to jam into place and pound until they held. A few times I had to push in a couple and wedge in a third. It wasn't a pure fix, but it would help the boat ride a bit higher on that side. There was not time for anything fancier.

I had done all I could there. I climbed out onto the shore and dripped. A pair of herring gulls dipped low near us and made their "kree, kree."

"What now?" Monique and John kept bailing. They had made visible progress. The boat rode higher and the water was below their knees in the boat.

"Palm fronds," Rolf said. "As many wide ones as you can."

A number of larger coconut fans of leaves lay on the ground near the dense green growth. I gathered these. I was not up to climbing a tree, and doubted if I could cut or pull the fronds loose if I could make the climb. I had a bundle of them in my arms and was dragging them back toward the boat when Jocelyn staggered into the sun-lit opening.

"Chancy?" I asked.

"Back there." She nodded toward the woods and nearly fell. The uzi hung loose in one hand.

I dropped my bundle and went to her, got an arm around her without pressing her wounds, and led her to the boat. She saw the condition of the boat. "That won't get us far."

"It doesn't need to get us far," I said. "Just away."

Rolf and John helped get her aboard. Monique stopped bailing for the first time and moved to help Jocelyn settle onto the seat behind the console. Ankle-deep water sloshed around in the boat. They had done some serious bailing. Rolf and Monique got back to it while I climbed off to go get the fronds. Haitian John got off the boat and limped after me to help. The wrappings on his feet were soaked. The trail of one wrapping dragged behind that foot as he walked.

We each took part of the bundle of fronds and started to the boat.

A shot sounded very close to us. Chancy backed out of the woods. He fired another time, then turned and ran toward the boat. "Come on," he shouted.

I ran with my bundle. Rolf and Jocelyn each had guns pointed toward the woods. Chancy stopped to look back and aim at something moving. He fired a shot.

I got to the boat, handed the fronds over to Rolf. Jocelyn fired a couple of times at something I did not have time to look at. I untied the rope holding the boat to shore and threw the end of the rope over on board.

Rolf was rigging a series of the fronds to the console, tying them into place with the balloon cord. The breeze caught at them and tugged, making them hard for him to wrestle them into place with only one good hand.

Chancy got to the boat and handed his gun to Monique. She and Jocelyn began to fire shots. A bullet whizzed past me and made a plop in the water ahead of the bow.

Chancy waded down into the water. "Got to push it off. Get away from the shore."

I got into the water by the stern. The bow was already nudging away from the shore, pulled by the wind. Haitian John was still not halfway to the boat, carrying his fronds with mincing steps. "Come on, John," I yelled. I got the rest of the way into the water and pushed against the starboard side of the stern. Chancy was in up to his waist pushing against the port side nearest the shore. "Drop the palm fronds. Run."

Flashes of light from shots came from three, then five places along the green wall of plants. Bullets that ricochetting off coral and stone whined past the boat. One clipped a palm frond in half as John dropped his bundle and shuffled forward as fast as he could on his bandaged feet. Monique and Jocelyn fired back at the woods.

Chancy sloshed up out of the water and ran toward John. High above us I became aware of a sound. It was the "whop, whop, whop" of a helicopter coming closer. The chopping whirled into an overpowering roar. A helicopter burst over the tops of the trees and swung in a tight circle over us. It lowered. Shots from the door-gunner sprayed into the jungle wall from where the shots were being fired. Bits of green chopped leaves, brown bark, and dirt flew into the air as the gun chattered.

All shooting at us from the forest stopped. The helicopter hovered and pivoted. There was a pause. Then bullets poured out from the copter's side again. I saw Chancy waving his arms back and forth as he ran. A line of bullet marks pinged and whanged off the ground in a trail that headed right for Haitian John. Shots ran across John's body, spinning him and nearly cutting him in half. He crumpled in a thin and twisted pile of brown arms and legs. Chancy got to him, looked down for only a second, then stood waving a fist at the copters.

The helicopter waggled from left to right. I could see the arm of one of the men waving. Then it roared off until it was lost to our sight. Waves smashed around me, and I was getting cold all the way through. The boat moved slightly farther out with each wave. I could hear more shots being fired in the thick green. The Bahamian Police Force had finally finished with Johnny Be Bad and had arrived to clean up Red Dreadman's posse.

Chancy turned and saw the boat easing away from the shore. He ran back and waded into the water. "Pull it back," he shouted.

I thought our chances would be as good on the water for a while.

The waves tossed the boat, making it hard to hold onto its sides. The wave sets were getting higher. The tide was rising. Chancy got between the boat and the shore as the boat bucked on a big wave. My head snapped out toward the deep and I found myself looking down into a dip of a wave, and then up a wall of water of the biggest wave I had seen yet, a real tsunami compared to the others. It swept toward the boat, the top a line of white foam, the wall of the wave a dark blue wall the glittered in the light from the sun that now hovered over the tops of the horizon of trees. "Chancy," I yelled.

The wave lifted the boat and slammed it against the rocks. I though I heard a loud "Umph" just as I was pounded under water by the wave.

The set had three more large waves, each banging the boat against the shore, then the waves were back into their regular pattern. The breeze caught the boat and tugged it away from the shore again.

I swam around to the side. Chancy had a hand up on the boat's cleat and hung in place. His face was red.

"You okay?" I shouted. His face turned to me. His mouth was puffed, but set, and his lips were held tightly closed – not good. "Hey," I shouted. "Up in the boat. Give me a hand."

Jocelyn's face came over the side. Then Monique's.

"Help me get him on board," I shouted. We were drifting farther away from the shore with each wave set now.

The two of them reached over the side. Each grabbed one of Chancy's arms at the wrist. They pulled and I pushed. The effort sent me completely under water. Chancy lifted up until his waist was on the gunwale. He was there when I bobbed back to the surface. The women's arms reached to grab him by the belt. They pulled him the rest of the way in.

The fighting had spilled over to the shore. I saw Jamaicans and the police exchanging shots. We were getting farther from the action. The Jamaicans were on the run and fighting with all they had left.

I grabbed at the useless motor and pulled myself up and over the stern. We were a ways from shore and moving along with the breeze. Our palm frond sail rustled. I flopped soaking onto the deck. The water was filling in again. Monique had moved to the bow and was bailing. Rolf sat beside her. He was locked into a thousand mile stare off at nothing. Chancy sat on the deck, his back against one of the rod racks. He had both arms folded tightly across his chest. Jocelyn sat beside him. He stared at her, but did not speak. It looked as if they had been arguing. She no longer tried to touch him.

"Is he okay?" I said.

She looked up at me.

Then I saw the small red bubbles of foam at the corner of his mouth.

To the West the sun slipped down into the trees in a line of pink, then red.

"Geez, tam, tam, tam, geez, tam, tam, tam."

"Can someone look at the goat man and turn down his motor?"

"There's some more blood by your mouth. You're hurt. That's why you're a bit snappish."

"I'm always cranky when I haven't had my coffee, or a meal, or, or, any bloody damn thing."

"You winced when you coughed too. Let me look at your ribs."

"Stay away from my ribs, Jocelyn. Just stay the...damn hell away from my...You know what happened that time with Adam and his bloody rib."

Chapter Eighteen

There was a roar in my ears. It was getting darker around us. The sky was a dull sheet of iron. The swells that lifted and dropped us were the color of darkened wet steel. I couldn't tell if the roar I heard was part of the sea, the hum of the distant helicopter, or if it came from knowing Haitian John was dead. I looked down at Chancy. He had not moved since being hauled aboard.

He let Jocelyn wipe the bubbles of blood from the corner of his mouth, but that was as far as he would go in letting her help. There was nothing in her kit that might help what he thought was wrong, what we all thought. When he coughed I had to look away.

Rolf gave a start – lucid again – and looked up at our position. We had drifted with the breeze and were getting farther from the shore with each wave. He stood and yanked the palm fronds loose and tossed them into the boat. They floated in the water that half filled the inside although Monique and I were bailing. The boat had a slight list to its damaged side.

"She can't take open seas, by geez-tam cracker box. Not like tis." He looked ahead. A point of land swept out at the end of Elbow Cay.

"Will we miss it?" I asked.

"Rolf gives even odds, either tam way." Rolf frowned back to where the battle had happened along the shoreline. "What happens to police?"

"They seemed caught up in the thrill of the chase," Jocelyn said.

"It's probably hard as bloody hell to make any sense of all that chaos back there," Chance said. His voice was like copper pipes being twisted into knots.

I looked at him. He seemed calm. Far too calm. I had to look up and away. The sun setting on the far side of the island cast a pink-edged purple aura over the dark swaying line of palm tops.

"That's a kind perspective coming from you," Jocelyn said.

"Leave him alone," I said. "I don't know yet if everything we did was a damned bit of foolishness, or if Chance here didn't just accomplish something back there." I fought with a twisting burr of raw emotion in my throat. I swung to Rolf. "Is there anything we can do?"

"Hope the tam wind changes," he said. "And bail."

"Isn't there a flare or anything at all we can at least use to. . .?"

"Been through all that," I interrupted her. "Jocelyn, what about Chancy?"

"There's not a lot I can do." She stood up from beside him. "And I don't know if he'd let me if there was something I *could* do."

"He's a scrapper," I said. "A fighter and a survivor. Don't say that. As competitive streaks go, he's a four-lane highway."

"Don't you both know, that it's rude to talk about someone right in front of them," Chancy said.

"It's okay," she said, "as long as we don't use the past tense."

"What the hell," he said. "At least the hostages are free."

Jocelyn said, "I can commend what you did. But I'll never forgive you for what you put her through." She nodded to Monique. "Her, Haitian John, and the rest of us."

"I can live without *your* forgiveness," he said.

I don't know how long I'd known it, but the contempt in his voice was what triggered my full realization of the role Jocelyn had played. Someone had blown the whistle on Randall, forced him to close down his illegal exotic animal operation in a deal with the U.S. feds and ATF who were after the Jamaican gun dealers. It was someone who knew him and his operation well. Maybe the one who had blown the whistle didn't know it would lead to all this. Who could?

"Randall is your husband?" I asked.

"Brother," she said.

"You ratted out your own brother?"

"Jerry?" Monique spoke. "Is anything the. . .?"

"He's the one behind all of this, isn't he?" I said. "He got in over his head, trading weapons and handling dope with the Rastas, then dealing in endangered species. Maybe he figured he could handle the Rastas, but I guess he didn't count on you."

Jocelyn spun on me, shouted, "I was just trying to stop him . . . for the animals."

"He seemed a civil enough chap to me," Chancy said.

"You want to know about Jerry Randall?" She turned to Chancy and her voice dropped lower, was icy, distant, the way it can get when someone has to tear loose a piece of herself to tell something. "I'll tell you. He's an adventure seeker and a great white hunter."

"Which you deplore."

"Just listen."

Chancy shut up.

"He got his start taking people out to hunt creatures the customer might not have a chance at in a few years – bighorn sheep, pronghorn antelope, mountain lions.

You've heard of them – they're all on the endangered species list now. The rarer the species, the more he charged. He kept track of the declining numbers so there could be more thrill for the customers. Jerry would have led a customer to shoot the last Dodo if there'd been any left. He had most of the kills mounted as trophies, like some early pagan man proud of his prowess, carrying out just the heads and leaving the carcasses for the vultures. Vultures like his customers, the almost very rich who are looking for that special thrill. They're privileged. Time's running out for some animals, but Jerry'd help them make sure they got their's before the law stepped in and said 'enough.' It was a race with him. Do you know how hard it is to shoot a bighorn sheep, or a pronghorn antelope? Let the word 'sheep' guide your thoughts on that."

It was the most I'd heard Jocelyn speak since meeting her, and it was an impassioned as anything anyone had said. But she wasn't done.

"I only went out to Jerry's place when he thought he was going to lose one of the animals. I did what I could, not condoning what he was going to do with them but fearful just the same for their lives. He knew that it compromised my principles to help him, but he didn't care. He used it – the emotional blackmail of being a sibling – and knew I wouldn't rat him out."

"He was wrong, of course," Chancy said, wincing at something inside as he spoke. "That's why you didn't like to stay at the house as a guest, eh?"

"You never got inside his house, saw the walls lined with game he'd killed just like his customers. He was a trophy collector, even seduced Monique, strung her along for a while before dumping her. I'm just surprised he didn't insist on having her stuffed and mounted and put in the den as well."

Monique dropped her bailer and folded her face into her hands. Her shoulders shook. Jocelyn sloshed over to her, went to put an arm around her shoulders. Monique jerked away.

"Let's talk about something else," Jocelyn said.

"I wonder what'll happen to him when his pals in the ATF show their true colors," Chancy said. "I suppose that's how he got off the island – about the only way I can figure."

"I don't know," Jocelyn said. "And I don't care."

That wasn't true. I knew her just well enough by then to know she spoke what was on her mind, when she spoke at all, and she had always spoken the truth, until now. This was the first she'd seemed to care enough about us to lie. I'd never had a brother, and couldn't know how I'd feel if I'd just betrayed him over something I felt mattered more than his life. But the inside of her head had to be a real battleground of self-doubt that was in stark contrast to the shell of the confident exterior she had been sharing until now – she was like Chancy that way.

Where I had thought Monique deep and complex earlier I'd erred. Jocelyn and Chancy were both able to leap forward in action, right or wrong, driven by their convictions – something about which I could only guess. I knew so little about anyone on the boat, Rolf, the lot of them, even myself. I did know that I was starting to look up to Joecelyn the way Monique did, and that made me feel what hurt Jocelyn more than I expected.

The boat rose and dropped, and the sky got blacker.

In mid-bail, Rolf stopped and stared down into the water in the boat.

"Is he any better?" Chancy asked.

"Don't ask me. I'm a vet, not a brain surgeon."

"Hey, goat man, you with us?" Chancy's voice was

louder.

"He comes and goes," Jocelyn said.

"Is it dangerous?"

"I said I'm no expert. But chances are he'll be fine if we get to shore and get help."

"If."

It was quiet in the boat for a while.

"Oh, Joc." Monique let Jocelyn put an arm around her shoulder.

Jocelyn said, "I do know that people with broken ribs pushed into their lungs *have* survived."

"That's a comfort," Chancy said.

The port side gunwale was lower to the water than the starboard side. Each wave slapping that side sent a spray of water to the deck. I said, "Chance, if I help you, do you think we can move you to the other side?"

He looked around the boat. "Sure."

I lifted him under the arms as best I could and dragged. He pushed with both hands. The water had been to mid-chest on him on the one side. On the starboard side it was still over his waist. I picked up one of the bailers and began moving water over the side.

"How long's that been with us?"

I looked up to where Chancy's head was pointed now. He could look out over the water. A fin swept by, went down, appeared again farther away.

"About the last mile," I said. "One or two of them come and go. Think some scent of blood is seeping out?"

"Could be," he said. "Damn shame we can't catch one of the sods. Hey. What did I do with those reels?"

The rods were still all on the boat, and a few of the reels, though they had been under salt water for a long while.

"The two Penns?" I said. "Last I saw of them you had

them at Randall's place after we left the Abaco Inn. I haven't seen them since."

"Shame to lose a couple of fine reels."

"Hell, it'll give you an excuse to buy tackle when we're stateside," I said.

He looked at me, dark as it now was in the boat, seeing if there was anything patronizing in the tone.

Rolf shook his head. He was lucid again and stared with a startled look over at the dark outline of the shore, at the point that stretched out as we got closer.

"Oh, tam. Oh, geez, tam, tam." Of all the things he had said, when he was in and out of his dotty spells, this made an ice cube scramble sideways up my spine.

The air was cooler and the water in the boat felt colder. I realized I had begun to shiver. "We going to miss it?" I asked.

"By a bit," he said. "But we miss her."

Jocelyn stood and peered.

Monique sat up straight. She was suddenly tough and ready again. "What can we do?"

"Can we turn on any of the boat's lights?" Jocelyn asked.

"Yust one light on console. I tink it don't work too good wittout power." He chuckled, an edge of hysteria to the chuckle.

"Maybe it needs to be changed," Chancy said. "Oh. What the hell was I thinking. It's got to *want* to change first."

There was a pause. Then Rolf laughed, out loud and for real. It was a good thing to hear. I was glad he was with us. I was glad Chancy was still alive.

"Oh, for Christ's sake," Jocelyn said. But she laughed too. They all kept laughing. It was the silly kind of limp joke that would be a raw flop at any other time. Maybe we were all exhausted, hysterical, stretched close enough to the edge to grab at it. Even Monique laughed. We'd needed something to ignite us and take away some tension. I was surprised it had come from Chancy and not Rolf.

It was getting dark in the boat. I had to squint to make out the others. To see land I had to stand, and was almost too tired to do that. Chancy cleared his throat.

"There is one thing I'd like to get off my chest."

"Hope it's not an excess of manly hairiness."

"Oh, come on," Monique said. "Let him talk."

"Go ahead, Chancy. What is it?"

Once encouraged, he seemed reluctant. In the dimming light I couldn't tell if he struggled with what he wanted to say, or the physical ability to say it. Then he was able to speak. "Sorry as hell for hazing you about the animals. You went through a lot, Jocelyn, and put up with a lot," he said, his voice hesitant, faltering. "You're a sport."

I doubt if it was what he set out to say, but it was hard with the rest of us hovering about like so many voyeur buzzards.

"I think I could have made it through my life without being a sport," she said.

"Well, you're one nevertheless."

"I think he's trying to say he admires you," Monique said, "even respects you, Joc. Though it could be just some schoolboy infatuation."

"Was it the myriad pools of my eyes, or my girlish and demure comportment?" Jocelyn asked.

"Geez tam, barf bag."

"Forget the whole bleeding thing."

"Admired me how, then?"

"You've been under a lot of pressure."

"And the rest of you haven't."

"More than we have. You've held up damned well,

through all of it. That's all."

"You know what I've admired most about you, Chancy?"

"No. What?"

"How very married you are. That always gives a girl comfort. You are still at the leash, aren't you?"

"Oh, quite."

"Geez. . ."

"Not another time, goat man. Go back into one of your trances."

I'd been meaning to mention to Chancy the conversation I'd had with Myrna. But now I wasn't going to. Sure, he'd had his eyes open when he wanted to rescue the hostages, and had strung us along in the bargain. But it's the kind of thing he'd have done anyway if he could, the kind of thing he'd always wanted to do all his life. I couldn't bring myself to look at him laying there so diminished. I said nothing about it.

It was quiet again in the roll and pitch of the boat over the swells and occasional wave. The breeze was steady, and all wrong for us.

I stood and looked. We were drifting along, getting nearer to the point, the last bit of land before we would head into the Atlantic. We could no longer hear shots, and there were no helicopter lights. The sea around us was all the steady slopes of swells. I didn't ask. Before anyone could speak I went to the stern, slipped off my shoes, stepped over the transom and dropped.

The water was damned cold. I went clear in over my head. It woke me a bit. I kicked back up until my head broke the surface, had to take a stroke or two to get back to the boat. I grabbed at the motor until I had a firm grip. Whatever I held felt greasy to the touch, but it was something to cling to with both hands. I began to kick as hard as I could, pushing the boat toward the shore.

Above the sound of my splashing, I heard a scuffle on board.

"Let go of me you bleeding goat sticker you."

"Hold him, Rolf." That would be Jocelyn. "You wouldn't be any good to us out there, Chancy. Please. Stop. You'll hurt yourself."

I kicked and was surprised I had anything left to kick with. I felt light as a feather, as surprised I didn't skitter across the waves like one of the downy feathers dropped from a herring gull as I was by having the power to kick.

"Look, Chancy," Rolf said. "By geez tam. We might make it."

I heard the sound of the surf, that and the roar between my ears. I kicked like a madman. The water did not seem cold now. It seemed warm, like the snow drifts where tired travellers in a storm lay down to sleep. Damn. That would be nice, wouldn't it. Pillows. A bed.

I felt one kicking leg slam into something hard and as raspy as file, thought for a second it was a sand bar, that we were that close to shore. The boat was turned enough now I could see the point. The boat was moving to the inside of it.

"We *will* make it," Jocelyn shouted. "Get him."

Something slammed into me. All I could think of was to keep pushing the boat and kicking. I was suddenly yanked under the surface. My whole body shook from left to right. I felt it now. My leg. The meat, the bone of it. Then I was free.

I bobbed to the surface, shot out to my shoulders. The boat had drifted from me. I tried to kick, couldn't. One leg worked. I used my arms in frantic long strokes. I could see the back of the boat, heads above the stern. I heard shouting, screams. I grabbed the motor, held tight.

Time went all elastic on me, like in one of those Japanese Noh plays, where the actors move in elaborate slow motion. I could taste metal, and salt. The water seemed very warm, almost hot. I thought I heard Chancy yell.

Something slammed into me, hard, smashed me against the stern. The water frothed around me. I felt the twisting, shaking pull on my other leg. I squeezed with all I had, clinging to the motor. My hands popped free and I was pulled under. The water closed over me. Now it seemed cold as I was pulled deeper. Very cold.

"Someone give me a hand. I've got him by the hair. Hurry. They're circling and coming back."
"I can't, Chancy. You Rolf?"
"Yust slow is all. Got an arm. Pull."
"He's alive."
"Get Jocelyn's kit, Rolf. Quick."
"Geez tam, Snickers bar."
"Hurry."

Chapter Nineteen

The small plane, a Cessna Conquest, dipped down out of the bank of wispy white clouds into the bluer sky that spread over the Atlantic. Its wings waggled left and right, the wing tips bouncing in the turbulence for a moment. The pilot didn't wear goggles and a Red Baron scarf slung over one shoulder, but he may as well have. He flew like he did. I had made this same flight on other small planes, Piper Cubs and the rest, many times. You take what you get in the way of pilots. Ours of the moment seemed to be having a serious World War I fantasy as we approached Abaco Island.

"It's beautiful."

I looked out my window and down to the flats Dawn was seeing. Small dead coral bits poked from the water, some stark and black, others covered with the green of stubborn mangrove and other tough tropical growth. It did look nice from up here, might even be nice down there pole-pushing a flats boat around and casting for bonefish.

Dawn leaned closer to me and slipped her arm through mine. We sat in the pair of seats directly behind the pilot and were the only passengers on this run. "Thanks," she said, "for bringing me here. How are you doing so far?"

"Fine." Three years had passed since I'd made it back.

I glanced at her, caught her in profile looking out her window. Her hair was the color of the often spoken of ripe wheat bending on a Kansas plain. A spray of freckles ran across the bridge of her nose. Chancy might have poked at me about her slightly recessive chin – had a bit of fun with that, and that Dawn was young enough to be my daughter, if I'd ever had children. Hell, I'd called her Hanna once or twice myself.

Below us, as the plane lowered and turned for its landing, I could see one or two of the wrecked planes that lined the strip. There were quite a few of them when I'd first landed at Marsh Harbour a few years back. It once gave me a thrill, even made me feel that there was some risk to flying in at this tiny airport. Now I just wished they would clear out the rest of the wrecks and let the green take back over where the tangles of white wings and busted red and yellow fuselages stuck out as color spots in the matted vegetation.

The landing gear hit, popped us a hop, then settled back to land. The whine of the engine slowed.

"Just think," Dawn said, "if you hadn't. . .I'm glad we met. I might never have seen all this."

I did think about it. I'd thought too much about it. None of the thinking had helped much. I forced my mind to the details of being helped from the plane and into the chair they unfolded. Getting our two small bags through customs took only a few minutes. We were the only ones on our plane.

Outside the one-building terminal, the taxis formed the usual line. I wheeled toward a minivan that was not first in the row, but looked like it could handle us better. Dawn had to break into a power walk with the bags to keep up.

The driver leaned against the side of the van. He pushed himself off the fender and towered over me, his large round black face stretched into a smile.

"To the ferry," I said, panting.

"My name's Big Deal," he said. His voice was like a train entering a subway. "What's your hurry?"

"Trying to catch the 10:15 ferry," I said.

"It's 9 a.m.," he said.

"Oh." It shot through me like a jolt of electricity that I was acting a bit like Chancy had.

Big Deal helped me in and tossed the bags in the back. He moved in a controlled and steady slow motion. He started the van, pulled out onto the road. His smiling face turned to look at us while he drove.

"We're on the wrong side," Dawn said. Big Deal snapped his head back to the road. He chuckled.

"It's British rules here, Dawn," I said. "Left side of the road."

"Gave me a start there," she said.

"This place takes a bit of getting used to," I said.

"You think so now," Big Deal rumbled, "you all should of been here a spell back. We had. . ."

"I heard about it," I said.

When we got to the ferry dock, we were, as Big Deal had said, way ahead of schedule.

"Plenty a time to enjoy," Big Deal said. "Catch you a taste of the breeze."

"Time for some Johnny Cake, too" I said. Dawn went to the small snack window and got us a slice from the vendor. She wheeled me out to the end of the ferry dock, where our bags waited. I looked out across the sound, could see Elbow Cay from here but none of its details. Dawn broke us each off a piece and we took bites. Far across the blue water we could see the ferry coming across toward us.

"Tastes like Bisquick," Dawn said, "but good."

I, for reasons I was not sure of, tasted breadfruit.

"What?" she said, looking at my face. "You don't resent my being here, do you?"

"No," I said. I looked around at the swaying coconut trees, the needle fish swimming below us, out across to where birds were turning.

"I think you're brave to come back here."

"Brave?" I said. There was no self pity in the huff of air I let out. "You can't find a piece of map in the world that doesn't have the footprints of one squabble or another running from one end to the other across it. The thing is how we weather it. I know that all my life I always ran, escaped, denied, every damn thing in my life. I don't know what I'd have done different if I'd had a choice. Maybe run. Who knows. Thing is, I didn't have a choice."

Dawn shuddered, then forced a smile. "Look. The ferry's here."

The Abaco Ferry swept us across the water toward Elbow Cay. It was a heavy vessel that made light of the white caps the wind was whipping up around us. The ride across was not a time to talk. The only other passengers, a young couple, glanced at where my legs ended almost at my waist. They looked away. There was the roar of the boat, and the sky to watch for gulls, the water to look across hoping to sight a dolphin. Dawn stood beside my chair, put a hand on my shoulder, and stared out across into a sky above the island that had only one or two small friendly clouds.

We all get swept up in things bigger than ourselves, unless we live in a hole, or on some remote and untouched island, and I have come to believe that there are none of those left. Some of us even try to do our small part when a crisis comes along.

I felt bad at first about Chancy. But maybe that's what he wanted, wanted much more than I could know. I know now that I admired that in him, that larger-than-life hunger to do the right and noble thing, even if his version was tangled in what it takes to be a man. That wasn't such a bad thing either. Men are men, after all, and women are women, whatever the squabble about differences. And as men went, Chancy went several to the dozen. Rolf, Jocelyn, Monique, and Haitian John too. I don't know how I had measured up. All that mattered less. I'm the one with the story. Maybe that's enough, to be the one with the story.

The red-and-white lighthouse seemed to rise out of the horizon and loom as the ferry slowed to pass the small house on Eagle Rock island. We eased through the no wake zone. I watched the small cottages go by, each with fresh paint. Shells dotted the small strip of beach and I thought I saw the tracks where a turtle had come to shore.

"It's everything you said it was," Dawn bent close and nuzzled.

"You should see how the air feels just after a storm passes," I said. "The black line of clouds easing toward the horizon, the sky still greenish yellow and strange until the sun begins to heat away the moisture."

The ferry dropped us off at the public dock by the Post Office. The pilot helped Dawn lift my chair, and then me up onto the pier. He handed up our bags. We stayed on the pier for a moment and looked around. The ferry backed and pulled away.

The last time I had seen Hope Town many buildings were blackened or levelled. Looking around now, it was hard to tell that anything had ever happened here to put a ripple in this tranquil scene. A lot of fresh paint covered what had to be new wood. Green was everywhere. The plant life had grown back – perhaps the best and quickest way to recover and hide what had passed here. I saw only a random scar on a tree here and there on the older coconut trees, and on one thick tree what could be a line of bullet holes.

The sun beat down on us. The sky was a cloudless

blue. A breeze behind us swept across the yacht harbor and stood the ship flags out at rippling right angles. In the shade beneath a tree and a bush, two dogs lay curled in fur puddles, panting and watching us. One was yellow, the other black. They were otherwise identical enough to be siblings.

"It's as wonderful as you said," Dawn sighed.

I didn't know why I felt as numb as I did.

Dawn lifted the bags. I led the way down the pier and along the sidewalk toward the Hope Town Harbour Lodge. Navigating the irregular sidewalk and pathways was different on wheels, but not beyond doing. I led us around the long way, through town and past the huge Banyan tree where metal fishing floats as big as soccer balls had been painted, each decorated in a different way and hung from the limbs as red, yellow, blue, striped, or checked Christmas balls in June. It made me glad to see the tree there, to know it had survived, though it had taken its share of hurricanes through the years as well.

We went by the small cottages, the tiny Methodist church where Vernon preached, the knee-high white wooden fences. We passed a small black and a white girl leaning their wide-tire bicycles against a fence. They chattered about something that had happened on their ferry ride to school that morning, something neither would recall a year from now, perhaps a month from now.

"When do we meet the others?"

"Later," I said.

The lodge was just ahead. Beside us, a wide native woman hung up white sheets on a clothes line. Her black round fingers snapped the wooden clothes pins in place. She sang and hummed as she bent to get another sheet from the woven reed basket.

A breeze caught the sheets and stood them out into

crackling ripples. High above us sea gulls turned in a thermal, swooping with wings as white as the sheets.

I recalled what it was like to lay down on linen that smelled of the sun, of the salt air, even of the fish and birds.

We checked in at the lodge, spent much of the day in our ground floor room, then went out to be beside the pool beneath the bending coconut fronds. The bright yellow, green, and blue harshness of the day was mellowing into pastel shadows of evening as we cleaned up and headed back to town. The sky was taking on bars of pink and iron blue. The sun was not too far from the horizon.

We went slowly. Dawn helped move the chair over a rough spot now and then, looked around in rapt glee. She bent and punched my shoulder with a playful swing. "We should have come here sooner," she said.

"There was that year in rehab." I felt strange and reluctant, like someone letting a stranger look on his nude wife. I shook myself. It was none of my island. Lots of people had been here long before me.

We came around from the sidewalk side of the Harbour's Edge restaurant.

"Is this the place?" she said, "With the great burgers?"

"Yes."

"And the fish?"

"They're probably still here too."

Her eyes were wide, sparkling, taking in every detail. In many ways she was quite different from Hanna.

"The fritters? They'll have the fritters?" she asked.

"I'm sure they will."

In the bar we let our eyes adjust to the cool shade. Casablanca fans turned slowly over our heads. I rolled to a stop, stared out at the tables on the deck. Jocelyn sat at one of the picnic tables. She was dipping a conch fritter into the orange sauce.

"What is it?" Dawn said.

I thought I had recovered enough to speak when I saw another face. Monique came around from the other street entrance. She went to Jocelyn's table, bent from behind her and kissed her on the cheek. She sat down on the other side of the table.

"What?" Dawn said. I had rolled back a foot.

"Geez-tam and cracker soup." My head swung. It was Rolf, carrying three moisture-beaded beers to the table in his one good hand. Monique looked up and cheered, made a noise she no doubt thought sounded like a goat.

"Clop. Clop," Rolf boomed. He put the beers on the table and plopped down beside Monique.

I felt a fist slowly clenching shut in my chest. Breathing became hard. It was what had made me reluctant to return to the city, had made me slow to come back here.

Calling them to meet had used up almost all the strength I had. Facing them like this, only part of a person. . .the thinking-too-much and remembering part at that. . . .

The light was dim where we were. They had not seen us. I turned the chair and started back out of the restaurant. A chill breeze gusted in a puff across the yacht basin.

Dawn was caught standing. She had to spin and rush to catch up.

"Are you okay?" Dawn asked. "I thought. . ."

I shoved at the wheels and rolled along the bumpy path outside.

"You know," I said. "It's our first night in town. Let's not settle for burgers. We can catch a water taxi and go across the harbor to Club Soleil."

Dawn let go of my arm, stepped back, then spun and

ran.

I started after her, slow at first, then faster when I realized she wasn't trying to be caught. I rolled down the sidewalk, a good half block behind her now.

She cut around a corner, out of sight. I got to the corner, Lover's Lane for God's sake, and turned to find her leaning against a tall wooden fence bleached silver. Above her head the bougainvillea was blooming in thick fuchsia-colored clusters. Her head was pressed against the planks of the fence. I reached up and turned her around, tilted her face to me. Her eyes were the same pale blue as the sky, though watery now. Her lip quivered.

"Tell me," I said.

"I know this place has its share of ghosts for you," she said. "But I'm with you now. Let me be here. Let me help. Use me."

"I don't deserve you," I said. I pulled her down close.

"Probably not," she mumbled, then managed part of a chuckle .

I pushed her back to arm's length, "Everything I told you about that happened here is over. It's in the past, like some bad dream. I don't know that I'm much better with dealing with the present, or the future. But the deal we have is that you get to help me with that. I need you for that. Okay?"

"Okay." She sniffed, but managed a smile.

I said, "I'm not all the way there yet, am I?"

"You're so very close."

"But?"

"You have so much to let go of."

"When I play back all that happened, so much of it was accident, chance. I can't see anything heroic in what I did, only brash stupidity."

She blinked, looked away, then back at me. Then her

head lifted and she looked out across the water. The light of the fading sun caught and flickered in the sheen of her eyes.

"Did you mean what you said back there? You really want to take that water taxi?"

"Yes." The word quivered. The ends of my fingers shook on the arm rests of the chair.

We made the radio call and got to the right pier and stood waiting on the taxi, the sun going the rest of the way down and lights coming on across Hope Town and in some of the boats that bobbed in the water in front of us.

"You sure you want this?" she said. "The others were expecting you."

As the air dropped a degree or two, Dawn stood close. When I didn't answer she asked, "You don't think you've fallen back into the same old rut, do you?"

"No," I said. "A new rut."

She gave me a gentle punch with her elbow. "But you never fell for your therapist before."

"No. I never did that." My eyes seemed stuck on the boats bobbing at their moorings.

She was quiet for a moment. I could see the taxi's lights start across the harbor coming our way. She said, "The memory plays funny tricks. You get tangled up in what you can forgive, forget. It's often what you tell yourself did or didn't happen that makes life easier or harder."

I looked around as the water taxi approached. "But it's the same old island I've always loved."

She reached down and held my hand. I flinched for a second, then relaxed. I looked up at her.

Her head stayed in profile. The pupil of one eye rolled to the corner, tracking me.

"Come on," she said. "We worked so hard." She

stared ahead at the approaching light and gave my hand a shake. "We've talked all this out."

I could hear scraps of music above the breathing of the ocean wind, but my own heart hammered louder, all out of rhythm with the wind and the tune.

"What I can't figure is how someone could go through as much as you have and get so little out of it."

"That's no way to talk to a cripple."

"I wasn't speaking to the physical side. That's as healed as it can ever be."

I didn't answer right away. The water taxi was nearly to the dock.

The tide had gone out far enough to show piles of "knocked" conch shells along the shore by the pier where we stood. They were pale and bleached in the fading light. On each shell a hole had been knocked into the tapered whorl so the muscle could be cut and the meat drawn out. They looked as empty and dead as anything can ever get.

Dawn gave my hand a squeeze. "It beats me how you can arrive at the grace of forgiveness about the sharks, the Jamaicans, every sticker that stuck you, and every vine that tripped you, but you can't do the same for yourself."

"You think that's it?"

"What you went through would confuse a clairvoyant, much less a person tottering on their feet." She gasped. "Oh, sorry."

I gave her hand a squeeze back. I looked out at the dark sheen on the water while she spoke.

"I never know how much I can trust a narrator of something I haven't seen with my own eyes," she said. "But, from all you've told me, I admire Jocelyn as much as Chancy. Strong as their opposing views were, they both had the capacity to change. Monique almost certainly had more to her than you could have unearthed with your clumsy ways then, and Rolf could be a clowning Dionysus or the serpent in the garden of Eden. But he's fresh and genuine in a way most of us can only envy. John, perhaps the noblest of all of you, is dead by the chance of the color of his skin."

My voice rasped out in a husky, harsh whisper. "Just knowing the lot of them makes me more humble than losing a couple of legs. I guess that's why it shames me to think of looking them in their faces again."

"I just hope you plan to emphasize the side of yourself *you* like," she said.

"I do," I said. "I will."

"Well, you won't do it on the other side of the water from the people you've been telling me about."

I didn't answer.

"Do you know what attracted me to you?" It was getting harder for her to talk. She had to squeeze the words out.

"My quick and light steps on the ballroom floor?"

"No. But it was your fragility." She covered over a pause by rushing on before I could speak. "I mean, you were so lost. You'd been pushed adrift of all the manly brainwash you'd gotten through all the years – and I don't mean just the blither about asking for directions, controlling the TV remote, whether the toilet seat is up or down, or even sorting the laundry. I mean you really had sold yourself that, no matter what, you didn't really *need* anyone else. Then you wake up and find out you *have* to depend on others. That had to crush you."

Now she paused, but I found I didn't have anything to say.

"It wasn't pity, Dave. I needed you to need me, and if I'd met you any sooner than I did, I don't know that you'd have been capable. Don't. . ." she choked on a word, "...don't slip away on me."

Sitting there by the water, I could smell and taste the salt in the air. It wasn't a whole lot different from the taste of the ocean when the shark had me and took me under. But, inside I was lifting, bobbing up to ride some ocean swell.

She got her voice back, though it was lower, and husky too, the words coming out like cloth tearing slowly.

"The consistent thing you've admired about all the ones you've told me about, most of all your pal Chancy, was that they were doers."

"Do you think I'm...?"

"What would Chancy do? Jocelyn? Rolf, for that matter?"

The fist in my chest was unclenching. I felt myself pulling open each curled finger.

"Okay." I let out a long breath. Energy rippled through me like a warm flush of blood to every remaining part of me. "You're right. Let's do it."

I waved off the water taxi that was almost to the dock, and didn't wait to see if he saw or not, but spun the chair and pushed hard at the wheels as we headed back across the wooden planks of the pier. She moved up to put a hand on my shoulder as I rolled.

"You're a wonderful woman," I said, panting as I pushed the wheels. "Do you think you can keep up?"

"I sure as hell can."

We had gone half a block when a man stepped out from the shadows and stood in our path. He wore deck shoes with no socks, khaki chinos, a white linen shirt. His face was tanned the color of a teak deck. The contrast made his smiling eyes glow like blue gems on fire.

I said, "Chancy?"

"What the bloody hell's keeping you? We've been

waiting at the Edge."

"I thought you. . .?"

"Was dead? Felt like it for a long time. Same copter took us to Nassau. Doubt you remember. You were out of it. But you haven't been keeping up with your pals either."

"I called Sid Appleblan. He said he wrote you off, hadn't heard from you in a year at the time I called." I had done little more than make that one call.

"And it'll be a cold day when he does. I was in a lung for a spell, learning to breath, learning quite a bit. Then there was one thing and another here with Joc. I tried to call you a few times, but you were out of the loop by then. Where did you end up?"

"Kansas City."

"Not much ocean there." One eye closed in a slow wink.

"No," I said. "No ocean."

"When you called the others," he said, "I asked them to wait to tell about me. I wanted to surprise you." He smiled. There were no longer lines across his forehead. It made him look like he had lost years. He was as relaxed as I had ever seen him. But that took nothing from him.

"Where have you been?"

"Living right here on the island. Married Jocelyn the same year Rolf came back to retire here. The goat world's loss there, you're thinking. Aren't you going to introduce me?"

Dawn stepped around the chair. "I'm Dawn." She gave Chancy a hug. "I've sure heard an obnoxious lot about you. I can tell you that."

Across Chancy's pocket a logo was embroidered: "The Haitian John Bonefish Camp." I pointed to it. "That the biz?"

"Yeah. Esther's a partner." Chancy stepped around

behind me and took the handles to the chair, began to move me forward. Dawn climbed into my lap, put an arm around my shoulder.

"Want to talk to you about that when we can slip away for a smoke. I can get Cuban cigars here. Cohibas, you name it."

"Talk about what?"

"I could use a good desk man, someone to handle the command module. Hell, don't answer now. But I've had ramps put in already."

"What do you say we go have that burger?" Dawn said.

"It's what I've always wanted to do."

"The burger, or live on the island and work with me?"

"Both."

MARSH HARBOUR, Bahamas – Rev. Vernon Malone, Elbow Cay, Abaco Islands, married his 300th couple in the top of the Hope Town lighthouse this past Sunday. A large number of Hope Town residents and guests joined the couple at the reception held at the Methodist Church. At the close of the reception, Rev. Malone shared his traditional, "Let them eat key lime pie."

About the Author

Russ Hall lives in a cottage on a lake in the Hill Country of Central Texas, where he writes, fishes, and reflects on how his life might have gone had he found honest work.

His other books include *World Gone Wrong*, *The Blue-Eyed Indian*, and *Wildcat Did Growl*.